# Protecting His Wolf

## Weres & Witches of Silver Lake
## Book 7

# Vella Day

Down on her luck and stranded in a town she's never even heard of, werewolf Lexi Laramie is on the run from her enemies. Fearing all is lost, Lexi puts her trust in a mysterious and sexy stranger offering to rescue her.

Immediately drawn to Lexi's sexy smile and intoxicating scent, Sam Pompley knows he'd do anything to protect his destined mate. Giving her a safe place to stay is an easy remedy. As Lexi and Sam grow closer, their attraction ignites. But when Lexi's past comes back, she refuses to put Sam's life in danger. Will she shatter her own heart just to save the man she loves?

*Beneath the calm and shimmering surface lie intrigue, power, magic, and danger.*
*Welcome to Silver Lake—where appearances can be deceiving, and what you see isn't truly what lies below.*

# Chapter One

*To learn about Vella Day's other new releases, contests, and find new authors, subscribe to her newsletter and get three free books!*
http://smarturl.it/o4cz93?IQid=MLite

*An Unexpected Diversion (book 1 of Hidden Hills Shifters)*
*Bare Instincts (book 2 of Hidden Hills Shifters)*
*Montana Desire (book 1 of Rock Hard, Montana)*

L EXI LARAMIE GROUND her teeth together. "Are you crazy? You have no right to sell me. It's barbaric!"

Bill Laramie lifted his hand and slapped her so hard across the face that she stumbled backward, slamming against the sharp edge of the trailer's kitchen counter. Pain shot up her spine, but she refused to show how much his actions had hurt her, both physically and mentally.

Lexi was so damned tempted to kill the bastard right here, right now, but she wanted him to suffer with the poor decisions he'd made in his life. Let the gambler he owed money to come after him and dole out his own brand of justice.

*Release me,* her wolf begged. *I can take him.*

*He's not worth it.*

Her dad was a wolf too, and while he had been strong in his youth, in his current drunk condition, he was a mere shell of a man. His once thick brown hair, now in need of a haircut, was peppered with gray. His broad shoulders were beginning to round from lack of exercise. She too had been devastated by her mom's death, but did she go out and get drunk and gamble every night? Hell no. She mourned her mom while keeping a job.

He raised his hand once more, but she wouldn't let him strike her again. She swiped the blood trickling down her cheek, ready to defend herself. Could she kill him? Probably. Her Wendayan mother had imbued her with great strength and agility. Deciding to use that talent instead of her ability to shift, Lexi executed a roundhouse kick to his midsection. As expected, the old man tumbled on his ass and landed with a grunt. Lexi stood over him. "Don't. Ever. Hit. Me. Again. You understand?" She refrained from saying what she might do if he did.

His eyes darkened with fury as he half rolled over. "You will pay."

"Me?" Lexi stepped back, clenching her fists at her side. "How much money do you owe this time?"

Her father lifted up onto his elbows. "Ten thousand dollars and he knows I don't have that kind of cash. Justin Kapok said we'd be even as soon as I hand you over to him. And don't think you can hide. The man has enough resources to find you no matter where you are."

Her stomach churned with a strong ache. Kapok was a known gangster in their wolf Clan. Months ago at a bar, he'd tried to convince her to hook up with him, and she'd said no. Apparently, that had been the wrong thing to say to such an influential man. That night he'd made it clear that his goal was to find a powerful mate to help him climb the Clan ladder—and she fit the bill perfectly. Asshat. He had bragged that once they were together, he'd have her popping out pups, one right after the other to increase the Clan's population. She wasn't against having a lot of kids—just not with him. For Justin, the concept of love seemed totally foreign to him.

"What possessed you to play poker with someone of that man's caliber?" she asked, aching in so many places, but especially in her heart.

"He asked me to play." Fear for his life suddenly replaced the angry lines around his eyes and mouth.

She loomed over him again. "I'm twenty-four years old. Last time I looked, human trafficking was illegal."

The dim light from the one lamp in the trailer's living room flickered, casting a sickening yellow pall over the room. Spittle dripped down her father's chin, but he didn't bother wiping it away. He rose to his feet, teetered, and then tapped her chest hard. "You're my daughter. I raised you, spent money on you. I can do whatever I want with you."

He was delusional. "You need help. Serious help."

Quicker than she thought possible, Bill Laramie grabbed her arm and shook her. Lexi had had enough of being manhandled. Stealing herself against the upcoming pain, she slugged him hard, and he folded like a weak collapsible chair. Damn, her hand hurt.

His head hit the stained carpet and his eyes rolled back in his head. He was out for the count. Good. Lexi should feel guilty that she'd had to resort to violence against her father, but if she hadn't defended herself, no telling what he might have done next. Probably tie her up and then call Justin to come get her, and she couldn't let that happen.

"You shouldn't have hit me," she said to the unconscious man. In her mind and heart, the pitiful person on the floor was no longer the man she used to care for. The man she remembered had been clean and funny. When he wasn't out working one of his two jobs, he'd played with her and her brother when they were growing up. What a shame that man had left this earth long ago.

"You are no longer my father. I'm leaving, Bill, and you will never find me." It didn't matter he couldn't hear her; she needed to say it.

Blood caused by the blow had congealed on her cheek, but right now she wasn't worried. Her wolf would heal her soon. With a heavy heart, Lexi spun on her heels and ducked into her temporary room at the far end of the trailer. She'd been stupid to agree to move back into his filthy hole in the wall last month, but Bill had been so convincing. He told her that with her help, he could clean up his act. What a crock. The man hadn't even tried.

Lexi quickly packed one bag. Less than five minutes later, she was out of there, not daring to look over her shoulder. Once outside, the cold Vermont air bit into her skin, but at least it convinced her she was still alive. It was close to midnight, and even though she had excellent shifter vision, she needed the moon's light to guide her, since her vision had blurred from the sheen of tears.

Unfortunately, as soon as Lexi slid into her 2001 Toyota Camry and twisted the key to start the engine, she flooded it. "Come on, come on."

After waiting a minute, Old Betty fired up and she took off. Lexi hadn't reached the edge of Windwood, Vermont before it occurred to her that while Bill wasn't savvy enough to find her if she charged down south, Justin Kapok was. Damn. Credit cards would leave a trail of her travel. That meant she'd need cash.

Slowing down, she fished her phone from her purse and dialed her brother's number. He answered on the second ring. "What's up, sis? Shouldn't you be in bed?"

"Funny." She didn't need to remind Ronan that her temporary teaching job had ended in December, and she hadn't found another position yet. "Look, I'm sorry to bug you, but I really need your help."

SAM POMPLEY HELD up his beer mug and tapped it against Connor McKinnon's shot glass. "To a job well done," Connor said. "Any time we take down a you-know-what, it's a good day."

"Amen." Sam tossed back his drink. Shouts from the back room echoed through McKinnon's Pub and Pool. Someone must have won a game.

Their case involved a Changeling who had tried to swindle one of the storeowners in town. The owner happened to be a fellow clansman of theirs, and he had immediately contacted McKinnon and Associates for help. After tailing the culprit for a few days, they'd caught the bastard with the stolen merchandise and returned it to the store. The best part was that they'd been able to bring the thief in, and he'd been arrested—not the usual end for a Changeling.

"For me, the game changer was when you were able to get close enough to the man to do a mind meld on him," Connor said as he set his empty glass on the bar top.

Sam leaned back and smiled. "I can still see the guy's face after he realized he'd led us right to the stolen compressors," he said before draining his glass.

Connor chuckled. "I bet the bastard will be pondering for years to come how that happened."

"That's why I love what I do."

They both laughed. Connor waved to his brother Finn, who was tending bar. "As much as I'd love to stay out all night and talk about our company's highlights, I have to be up early. From the sounds of the winds out there, a winter storm is rolling in, and I don't want to get caught in it like I did that one time last winter."

"I thought you enjoyed romping in the snow." Connor was a werewolf.

"I do, but it's not smart to attract attention in the middle of town."

Sam wasn't a shifter, but he understood the need to be circumspect. "We see wild animals crossing the street from time to time. I don't think it would attract too much attention if you hoofed it."

"You'd be wrong. People think bears are cute, but wolves? They're touted as a menace to society because they eat the farmers' chickens. It's not like I haven't been mistaken for a real wolf and been shot at."

"That would suck."

Finn waltzed over, and Connor slapped a twenty on the bar. "You leaving so soon?" Finn asked.

"Work calls or rather my bed calls. This should cover both our drinks. Keep the change, little brother."

Finn grinned. "Thanks."

"You didn't have to do that," Sam said.

Connor clasped a hand on Sam's shoulder. "You deserved it after helping catch that thief."

Sam slid off his stool. Both of them had parked in the alley in back because all the close spaces up in front had been taken. Bad weather always brought people inside. As they stepped out back, a strong blast of wind snaked up Sam's jacket, forcing him to button up. A scraping sound in the direction of the dumpster caught his attention. "What's that?" he asked.

"I sense a shifter." Connor stopped, looked around, and then headed in the direction of the noise.

The wind whipped around the alley, lifting the snow covering the ground and shooting swirls into the air. Unfortunately, the fresh air wasn't enough to mask the stench of the trash. Sam caught up with Connor just as he lifted the lid of the big trash bin.

"What the hell?" Connor said. "It's a female wolf. At least she's small enough to be one."

Sam peeked in. A small wolf was inside, her face smudged with some kind of food goo. Her eyes widened, and then a low throaty growl escaped. While Sam wasn't a shifter, he knew that werewolves or any kind of shifters didn't dumpster dive. "What are you doing in there?" he asked, knowing full well he wouldn't receive a response.

Connor nudged him. "She's obviously hungry."

That much Sam had figured out. During his many tours in Afghanistan, he'd seen hunger, and it tore at his heart every time. He addressed the pretty wolf with the gold and brown snout. "If you shift, I'll buy you dinner."

The wolf shivered and then bared her teeth in a highly aggressive manner. Not to be deterred, Sam edge closer, and the poor creature backed up despite having little room to maneuver. While he was no shifter expert, from her body language, he could tell the poor thing was scared.

"If she shifts, she'll be naked, and I doubt she'll like that," Connor said.

Sam hadn't been thinking. He whipped off his jacket and placed it on the rim of the dumpster, trying to ignore the brutal cold seeping into his skin. "Put this on and then come out."

He nodded at Connor that they give her some privacy, and they then jogged back to their respective vehicles. As Sam unlocked and then slipped into his four-door truck, the jacket disappeared. He started the engine and turned the heat to high, watching and waiting. A minute later, a petite woman crawled out wearing his camouflaged wool Pea Coat. The fabric covered her butt, but not much else, causing something inside him to spark. What the heck was that about? Okay, those legs of hers were attractive, but enough for a blue spark to fly off his hand?

She darted down the alley to an old Toyota Camry, and he winced at what it would be like running barefoot. While it was lightly covered in snow, rocks protruded randomly, making the way painful. Their dumpster girl, however, acted as if she was moving across a soft carpet. When she reached her car, she grabbed a handful of snow and rubbed it over her face to clean it. Once she finished doing the same to her hands, she jumped in the back of her car, hopefully to change.

A few minutes later, a knock sounded on his window. The woman was holding out his jacket. Instead of lowering his window, he pushed open the door, and she jumped back.

"Thank you," she said before turning away.

Sam snatched his coat, slipped his arms in the sleeves, and jerked it up and over his shoulders. "Wait. My offer still stands to buy you dinner."

She shook her head. "I'm not fit company."

Connor's door eased open, and he stood next to his car.

"Where are you staying?" Sam asked in as non-threatening a tone as possible, hoping she didn't say her car.

She wrapped her arms around her shoulders and rubbed them. Thankfully, she wore a down jacket and a wool cap. "I'm just passing through."

"That didn't answer my question. You have to sleep somewhere." If she owned a car, why was she looking for food in a dumpster? Her speech sounded educated, so she probably wasn't a thief. "Do you need any money?" Sam pulled out his wallet and extracted the only two bills in there. "Here's forty bucks. Go buy yourself some food."

"I can't. Thank you though."

Before he could stop her, she ran off and hopped into her car. Normally, he would have shrugged, content that he'd tried to help, but something about this delicate creature spoke to him. He refused to address how his sexual interest had flared. It must have been that second beer he'd had.

"What's she doing?" Connor asked as he stepped next to him.

"Leaving, I guess. I tried to give her money, but she wouldn't take it." Her engine sputtered, and then the car chugged a few feet and died. She slapped her hand on the dash then lowered her forehead to the wheel.

"I'm going to see if she needs help," Sam said.

Connor reached out to stop him. "Let her come to you. It's less intimidating for her that way."

His friend had a point. "I'll give her a few minutes, and then I'm stepping in." While he hadn't been a mechanic in the service, he knew his way around a car engine.

They returned to their warm vehicles and waited. Sure enough, five minutes later, their little dumpster girl stepped out from her car, the wind buffeting her so much she had to battle against it.

As much as Sam wanted to shield her from the weather, he believed what Connor said; their little wolf needed to approach them. This time when she knocked on Sam's window, he rolled it down. "Change your mind?"

"Kind of, since my car seems to have run out of gas."

He didn't need to ask why she didn't buy some more. "The offer for money still stands."

She pressed her lips together. "How about that meal instead? It's hard to think on an empty stomach."

"Sounds good. My name's Sam by the way. Sam Pompley."

"I'm Lexi Daniels."

"It's a pleasure to meet you, Lexi. How about getting in while I speak with my boss? I think I know of a way to help you."

"Your boss?"

"The other man; his name is Connor McKinnon." He nodded to Connor's car. "I work for McKinnon and Associates. We're a security agency." Her eyes glowed, implying she might be on the run and could use someone to look after her—or else that had been wishful thinking on his part. He stepped out, walked around to the other side, and held open his truck's passenger door. "Hop in. I'll get your luggage."

Wolf lady sucked on her bottom lip as if she couldn't decide whether to trust him. "Why are you doing this?"

That question took him by surprise. "Because I'm a nice guy?" Her eyes narrowed and he continued. "I just returned home after several tours in Afghanistan. Helping others is ingrained in me."

Her shoulders seemed to relax. "What about your boss?"

She was cautious, and he liked that. "He's a good guy. Trust me."

The wind howled and more flurries fell. "Okay." She slipped into the front seat but kept her gaze on him.

Sam hoped he was doing the right thing in wanting to give her shelter, praying the Changelings hadn't sent someone as lovely and vulnerable as this woman to infiltrate their camp.

# Chapter Two

WITH LEXI'S LUCK since she'd left Vermont, these men couldn't possibly be as nice as they claimed. She'd already been fooled once on the way down here. Connor was a shifter like herself, which in itself made her suspicious. What were the odds of another shifter finding her? At least she hadn't run into someone who believed she was a regular wolf. That person might have tried to capture her and keep her in a cage—or worse, killed her.

Each man was hot as hell and made the coincidence seem even more improbable. Connor was about the same height as Sam but not as beefy. Both had rather short dark hair, but it was Sam's straight nose and full lips that really appealed to her.

*Stop it.* What was she doing thinking about these men like that? She was here for a meal and then she had to move on.

The huge man with the thick hair returned after speaking with his boss, climbed in the front seat of his truck, and then turned toward her. Her pulse soared and a random blue spark shot off her hand. What the hell? Sure, he smelled divine—though anything would smell good compared to the garbage stench she wore. Besides, being excited had no place in her life—now or in the future— especially since she was running for her life.

"I just spoke with my boss and he's okay with you staying at our safe house if you'd like. You can clean up before we grab some food."

Lexi hadn't eaten in twenty-four hours and was starving. It was why her brain cells had short-circuited. *Go for it,* her wolf urged. *I like him.*

"That sounds too good to be true," she told Sam. For once, Lexi agreed with her wolf and decided to follow her gut. These two seemed to be on the up and up. Besides, she'd never felt grimier in her life and couldn't think about eating until she showered and changed. She didn't know how this man wasn't gagging.

The second man waved as he got into his truck and drove off.

Lexi was totally ashamed at having these men see her stoop so low, but she'd been desperate for food that when she spotted the dumpster, she thought she'd check out what the restaurant had thrown away. The smell of pizza had enticed her. Boy, had that been a mistake. She was so lost in her head that she didn't realize Sam was speaking to her. "I'm sorry, what did you say?"

Sam gave her a kind smile that showed he knew she had been off in her thoughts. "I just asked where you're from, Lexi."

"Up north."

She glanced over at Sam cautiously. Could he tell she didn't want to give away a lot of information? It didn't matter. She'd shower, eat, and then decide what to do. Of course, with no money and a broken down car, her options were limited, especially since she was stuck in this town with a blizzard threatening to block all the roads.

"I see."

"What's the name of this town anyway?" she asked.

"Silver Lake."

She'd never heard of it. While she considered asking if there was a shifter community here, she decided against it. Lexi could tell he wasn't a shifter and even though his boss was one, she couldn't risk saying anything if Sam didn't know that. Obviously, he was aware she was one. *What am I doing?* It wouldn't matter if there was a community or not since she'd be leaving soon.

As they headed away from town, the storm intensified and buffeted the truck. Less than five minutes later, he pulled in front of a building that looked like a fortress. Made of cement, it sported few windows—at least on the street side. No other buildings were close, which could be good or bad, depending on the circumstances.

"This is our office, which has a safe house underneath it, along with a few spaces underground for parking. There's also a large gym." He waved a hand. "Never mind. I don't know why I even mentioned it. I doubt you'll want to use it. You can crash in the suite for however long you need."

The words *safe* and *house* had her heart jumping for joy—as did the concept of staying in comfort for a few days—in a suite no less. If by some chance word got back to Justin Kapok she was staying there, being hidden underneath this large structure would be fantastic. "I really appreciate it."

Sam parked outside and grabbed her suitcase. "Wait here for me for a second while I open up. I don't need you to freeze."

While he was being very chivalrous, she didn't want him to think she was a wuss.

"I'm good."

She followed him to the front door, trying to ignore her cold and tired body that was begging for some nourishment and rest. He pressed his thumb on some kind of entry scanner, and the front door clicked opened. The moment she stepped inside, her muscles relaxed. Perhaps it was because the room smelled clean and felt safe. The overhead lights automatically flooded the space with light, giving her a chance to check it out. The warm, contemporary furnishings in no way matched the sterile exterior.

The taupe walls, gorgeous large photographs of a mountain range in the fall, and divinely luxurious light yellow sofas really drew her in, as did that thick white area rug. Oh, how she craved to walk barefoot on it. "It's beautiful."

"We like it. Connor's father, and the father of one of our deputies, built the place. It's totally state of the art. Hell, they have technology here that surpasses what I had overseas in the service."

Lexi barely listened to what he said. Instead, she enjoyed the way he spoke. His voice was so soothing; Sam Pompley would make a great radio announcer. He led her through the entranceway into a large room that seemed to be separated into two areas. Sofas and chairs were clustered on one end, though she wasn't sure of their purpose other than it being a place to hang out. On the opposite end was a long wooden table that sat eight. It was across from a kitchenette with a coffee bar.

"The entrance to the safe house is down here," he said.

As they entered the hallway, more overhead lights automatically flickered on. Nice. He wasn't kidding when he said this place was state of the art.

Sam opened a door near the end of the corridor then stepped into an office. A desk faced the entrance and had a bookcase behind it. Two leather chairs sat off to the side of the desk. While there was a computer on top, it was rather sparse—no desk clutter and no artwork on the walls. If this was Sam's office, she would have thought he'd at least have photos of him with his unit.

"This is our spare office. Connor's brother Devon works in another state, and if we have to call him in to help, this is where he works.

That explained a lot. "It's nice, but I thought you said there'd be a shower I could use."

Sam smiled, and her body nearly exploded with desire. Her bones even started to crack. What was up with that? Clearly, she needed coffee and food to help clear her head.

"Watch this." He moved three books on the fourth shelf to expose a button. As soon as he depressed it, the bookcase hinged open to reveal a stairwell. "The safe house is down here."

Wow. Had the short entryway not been flooded with light, she might have balked. "It looks safe."

"No one can get to you, I promise. We have motion sensors and cameras, but only in the hallway. You'll have total privacy in the suite."

When he'd first used the word suite, she'd blown it off, thinking he was being generous with his usage. Now she wasn't sure, though she was convinced something had to be wrong with this whole setup. What were the chances she'd break down in a town of shifters—well, at least one shifter—and then be saved by two hunky men, one of whom was doing something to her insides. Her wolf was overjoyed being near Sam that was for sure. For most of her life, her animal kept quiet. Why did she have to wake up now?

*Mate, mate*, her wolf cried.

*Nonsense.* Her mind had to be playing tricks on her.

Besides, staying in one place for long wouldn't be smart. However, she had to earn some money to at least pay for gas and food—enough to get her to Florida where she planned to hide.

"Here you go," Sam said as he pushed open the door.

Once more the lights flicked on, and her pulse soared. This was a dream. It sure as hell was nicer than any place she'd ever lived. It appeared to be a one-bedroom apartment, complete with a small kitchen and a living room with a huge flat screen TV. "This is amazing. Who stays here?"

"Our clients who need to hide, but you'll be our first guest."

Having such a large television along with a kitchen she didn't have to share would be a luxury. Any income she had earned teaching went to living expenses and then to helping her dad survive. Now she could see that had been money down the drain.

"Go ahead and shower then meet me upstairs." He set down her suitcase.

"Thanks." She was still unable to believe how nice the place was.

As soon as the door closed, Lexi spun around, not believing her good luck. The gods surely must be looking down on her. Hell, with her newfound luck, maybe she should take Sam up on his offer of forty dollars and buy lottery tickets!

Lexi peeked inside the bedroom, never expecting the king-sized bed and the all-wood dresser. The teal bedspread came with four large pillows and screamed comfort.

How much did these men charge their clients to stay here? The accommodations were nicer than nice. Oh, right, it was a safe house.

The cold and hunger were messing with her.

After placing her suitcase on the bed, she stepped into the large bathroom. The shower floor was made from river rock and three of the sides were covered in a copper colored tile. The fourth was a glass door. An inset shelf had shampoo, conditioner, and soap. While Lexi had never been to a spa, she suspected this was what it would look like. The stack of white fluffy towels only added to the luxury.

Not wanting Sam to wait too long, she turned on the shower then ditched her stinky clothes. Seconds later, steam rose. Really? They had a tankless water heater? It was something her mom had always dreamed of having.

The moment Lexi stepped under the hot flow, she moaned at the intense relief coursing through her body. As much as she wanted to stay there for hours, enjoying the heat, her stomach was urging her to hurry.

Ten minutes later, she stepped out of the shower and toweled off. The hair dryer attached to the wall was a godsend. After absorbing all that heat from the shower, she'd finally warmed up. Her straight brown hair was long, but not thick, so drying it took only a few minutes.

Even though she'd put on her clothes after having been in the dumpster, they still smelled bad. Lexi was tempted to trash them, but she didn't have enough to spare. For the time being, she let them soak in the sink, hoping it would help.

After pulling on a clean pair of jeans, a plain T-shirt, and a sweatshirt, along with her boots, she rushed upstairs to the main room. As she was about to pull open the door, she sensed another shifter. Her first jumbled thoughts imagined it to be Justin Kapok, until she remembered that the other fellow with Sam could shift. In fact, he ran the place.

Blowing out a breath, Lexi stepped through the vacant office and then into a hallway that smelled of tomato sauce and cheese. She almost melted on the spot.

Driven by hunger, she rushed down the hallway. Both Sam and

the owner—what was his name? Conrad? No, Connor. Both sat at a table with several pizzas in front of them.

"You're looking better," Connor said with a smile.

"I feel a lot better. The hot shower was divine, thank you."

Sam stood and pulled out a chair next to him. "We thought it would be easier and faster to bring the food to you."

Now she knew she was in a dream. These men were too good. What a shame she had to keep moving, but she couldn't chance Justin finding her—and find her he would. Not only had he paid for her, he wanted her for the healthy continuation of the Clan.

For now she needed to push those ugly thoughts aside. Lexi dug in, and the men each grabbed a slice.

"Sam tells me you're from up north. Which part?"

Lying went against her grain, but a little fudging wouldn't hurt. "New Hampshire." Vermont abutted it, so it was only a small lie.

"Nice. What brings you down this way, especially during snow season? The roads are often impassable."

Perhaps it was the warmth from the shower or the food that made her willing to talk, but she wanted to tell them something that wasn't a lie. "I'm kind of running away from someone."

Both men's faces turned dark. Sam placed a hand on her arm and heat seared her insides. Okay, that wasn't good. What was it about this man that had her off kilter?

*Mate!* her wolf said once more.

She almost snorted. Lexi was never that lucky.

"Did he hurt you? Is that where you got that bruise on your cheek?" Sam asked.

On instinct, she touched the spot where Bill had slapped her. Her wolf had healed the cut, but not the bruise. "It wasn't him. My father did this."

If they were working for Justin—which she figured was a super low possibility—then they'd know everything anyway.

"Care to explain? If you're in trouble, we can help," Sam said.

What did she have to lose other than some dignity? "It started about a year ago. My girlfriends and I went to a bar to celebrate one friend's birthday. As the night progressed, I drank a bit too much—even for my shifter metabolism. The birthday girl wanted to dance. I agreed. Next thing I knew, I was in the arms of a werewolf by the name of Justin Kapok. Sure, he was charming, but something about him had my sixth sense acting up."

"Was he a creep?" Connor asked.

"Yeah. He's rich and a very slick creep." She explained how he told her that he wanted to improve the bloodline of the Clan by adding a Wendayan mix to his wolf breed—namely her DNA. "Telling me he was interested in what I had to offer really turned me off. All he wanted was a brood mare. He assured me I'd have all the creature comforts I could possibly want, but material things aren't what I need." She needed someone to love and someone to share things with.

"May I ask what your specialty is?" Sam asked. "I'm a Wendayan too."

Lexi's pulse sped up. Being in the same room with a werewolf and a Wendayan was a rare event. At least now she was free to talk about shifters, since Wendayans and shifters were aware of each other. "I'm stronger than many men, and I'm rather coordinated, which has come in handy when fighting. I can be in my shifted form or my human form, and my magic remains." She held up her hands. "Just because I can fight doesn't mean I do very often. I try to avoid conflict whenever possible." She faced Sam. "What can you do?"

"It's hard to explain, but I can implant thoughts into people's heads and make them think things are one way when in reality they aren't."

"That's kind of creepy." She hadn't meant to scrunch up her face; it just happened.

He shook his head. "Trust me; I only use it to foil the bad guys."

That was cool and yet still kind of creepy at the same time.

"Do you think this Justin guy will come after you?" Connor injected, probably wanting to divert her thoughts from Sam's strange talent.

"I don't know if he realizes I'm missing yet, but when he figures it out, he'll come find me and drag me back to Vermont. My dad said as much."

"Vermont? Is that where he lives? I thought you said New Hampshire."

Damn. She always sucked at lies. The truth would be easier. "I wasn't thinking. I went to college in New Hampshire. We now both live in Windwood, Vermont—or rather that is where I used to reside." She explained that after her mom died, her dad went downhill, drinking and gambling, so she moved back home to help him out. "Apparently, Justin lured my dad to the poker tables, and he ended up owing Justin ten grand. He said that if my dad agreed to hand me over to him, they'd be square."

Sam's eyes seemed to change color and his teeth clenched. "He can't do that!"

"I know. I tried to explain that to dear old dad and got this for my effort." Lexi pointed to her cheek then placed her hands under the table and rubbed her knuckles. They were still sore from where she'd hit him.

"Are you saying your dad might come after you too?" Connor asked.

She shook her head. "He can't stay sober enough to drive out of town. No, if anyone comes, it will be Justin."

"When did this happen?" Sam asked.

"Last night." She held up her bruised knuckles. "Bill hit me and then I hit him back, hard. After he passed out, I packed a bag and ran. Not wanting to leave a credit card trail, I called my brother and borrowed five hundred dollars in cash from him." She held up a hand. "I know, I know. How could I blow that much money in one day? I was robbed on the way here."

"Robbed?" Connor practically growled.

"I'm still so embarrassed—and pissed. My engine was knocking, so I stopped at a rest stop to check it out. I was looking under the hood when two rather cute guys came over to see if they could help. While I was listening to one of the men's theory about the cause of the problem, it gave the other guy the chance to slip my wallet out of my purse that I had stupidly left on the front seat of my car."

"And they drove off, leaving you without any money," Sam added.

"Yes. I did have a twenty dollar bill stuck inside a zippered pocket, which I used for gas."

"That's a real shame." Sam pushed back his chair. "More coffee?"

"I'd love some." She was thankful they didn't give her a lecture about being careless.

While he carried all three of their mugs to the coffee station for a refill, Connor leaned back in his chair. "What are your plans now?"

"Sleep?"

Connor chuckled. "And afterward?"

"Head south where it's warmer."

Sam set her refreshed cup in front of her. "Before you were basically forced out of your home, what did you do for a living?"

"Since September, I was a substitute high school math teacher, but the regular teacher came back from maternity leave last week, which means I'm back to looking for a job."

"A math teacher?" Connor shot Sam a look she couldn't identify.

"Yes, why?"

"How are your computer skills?"

Where was he heading with this? "My programming skills are limited to easy HTML, but I'm a whiz at spreadsheets and word documents. Why?"

"The way I look at it, you need money and we need a secretary," Connor said.

# Chapter Three

L EXI WAS SPEECHLESS and nearly choked on her coffee. Were they offering her a job? Maybe she had been transported to a different realm—albeit still a cold one. "I admit I'm strapped for cash, but I don't plan to stay very long. You should give the job to someone who needs it."

"And you don't?" Sam asked.

He had her there. "I mean I do, but I don't need much to drive to Florida." She'd have to find a job once she arrived down south though. Her teaching certificate didn't extend to Florida, so she'd have to find something else.

Sam glanced over at Connor who imperceptibly nodded. "Then stay for just a while—until we find someone permanent. We just moved into this building and really need a person to answer the phone and relay messages in a timely fashion," Sam said. "Besides, you'll be safe here."

There he went again dangling that *safe* word. Her first instinct was to ask him once more why they were being so nice, but when her mother was alive, she had always said to accept gifts graciously. It was insulting to turn a person down when they were trying to do something for you.

"Thank you. I accept."

Both men smiled. "Good. I'm not sure about the shifters in New Hampshire, or rather Vermont, but for the most part here in Silver Lake, humans aren't aware of them, so you'll have to be careful what you say," Sam said.

"You don't have to worry about me. Unless I'm in the presence of my Clan, I say nothing."

"Perfect," Connor said. "To ensure your safety, do you think you can get a picture of this Justin guy in case we spot him in town?"

"I can try. He's often in the news. If not, I can ask my brother to find something and email it to me."

"Have him email it to us at the firm so there is no trace."

She hadn't been thinking. "Of course." The food, coupled with the lack of sleep was getting to her. Lexi yawned. "I'm sorry. If you don't have any more questions, I'd like to hit the sack. I promise I'll be more alert tomorrow."

Sam pushed back his chair and stood. "Do you need anything?"

She smiled. "I'm good."

"Then goodnight."

*Hug him*, her wolf said.

Yeah, right. The last thing Lexi needed was to become too attached, especially to someone as hot as Sam. If she had to relocate, it would be to a beach town, not to a place similar to where she'd come from.

"WHAT DO YOU think?" Sam asked Connor as soon as he heard the office door close.

"Think? She's a woman on the run who needs our help."

Sam was relieved to know his boss was on board with giving her protection. Thankfully, Connor didn't insist she pay for their services—not that she could anyway. It wasn't like she was a client asking to be protected. "I agree. Here's the strange part. I respect people's privacy and don't go mucking around in their heads, but I couldn't help but try to read her mind."

Connor's brows rose. "That's not like you, but what did you learn?"

"Nothing."

"What do you mean nothing?"

"Because I thought it was possible that the Changelings sent her to infiltrate us, I tried to give her some suggestions, but she didn't respond."

Connor stiffened. "Back up a minute. You think she's a Changeling?"

"No, but I didn't want to dismiss the possibility. It would be like them to stoop to something this low. When I attempted to make her think something was different than it really was, I failed."

Connor watched him for a moment. "I thought you could do mind control on anyone."

"I can, with one exception. From what I've been told, I can't get into the head of my mate."

His chin tucked under. "Your mate? Are you serious?"

"Crazy, right? Not only is she blocking me out, my whole body started to vibrate the moment I was near her."

Connor shook his head. "I wouldn't jump to conclusions yet. You probably can't get into James's head either, and he sure as hell isn't your mate."

Sam waved a dismissive hand. "He's an immortal. I'm talking about regular humans here."

"Who told you that?"

"My grandfather; we both have the same talent. He passed away a few years ago, but when I was young, he mentioned it. I swear he said that if I met a woman and couldn't read her mind, or affect her in any way that she was my mate." If the physical attraction hadn't been so strong, he might have dismissed it.

Connor picked up the last piece of pizza and wolfed it down. "I'd give it a few days and see what you think. Personally, I don't think she is. Being a werewolf, she'd know if you were her mate, and if she were, she wouldn't be claiming she wants to leave."

"Then what should I do?"

"If you're sure, then I guess you need to follow her to Florida," Connor said.

She did seem determined not to stay. "Maybe I need to convince her that Silver Lake is her destiny, and that I'm the best thing since sliced bread."

Connor cracked up. "I like it. I just hope this mate stuff isn't contagious."

"Your day will come."

"Not for many years, I hope." Connor washed down his pizza with the last of his coffee. "Far be it from me to stand between a man and his destiny. I'll ask Devon if he's free to fly to Vermont and check out this guy Justin Kapok."

"Really? I know Lexi would be thrilled not to have to look over her shoulder the rest of her life."

"No promises, but in the meantime, Jackson can do some research on this guy."

Connor pushed back his chair. "I'll ask him to get on it tomorrow morning. You can head on out. I'll lock up."

"I'll crash on the sofa. If Lexi wakes up and comes upstairs, I don't want her to be afraid."

His boss chuckled. "Give the girl a break, will ya?"

"Now that's insulting. I respect women. I want her to feel safe, that's all."

Connor failed to keep the smile off his face. "Make sure you get some sleep." With that he left.

Sam should be tired, but he wasn't. Lexi had jacked up his hormones to the point where he might never fall asleep again. Even if he wanted to crash, the Marines had taught him to stay awake when he needed to accomplish something—like getting the dirt on Justin Kapok.

Ducking into his new office, he fired up his computer. Jackson was the real genius when it came to research, but Sam wanted to do a quick search first. Connor didn't need to be wasting the company's resources with a non-paying client, so the more he could do, the less impact it would have on McKinnon and Associates. The fact Connor considered asking Devon and Jackson to help was amazing.

In the search engine, Sam typed the man's name followed by Vermont, and several hits appeared, one of which was a picture of Kapok wearing a nice suit standing alongside a Ferrari. That wasn't what Sam expected. It made sense though he'd be rich if he succeeded at gambling, but this rich?

The next shot was of Justin smiling. The fact he was a good-looking man bothered Sam. Jealousy had never played a role in his life, but right now, his blood pressure was rising. He needed to remember that the man was scum, looking only to improve his position in the Clan. Sam had learned that ambitious men with money had the reach to obtain what they wanted. No wonder Lexi was scared of him.

After another hour of digging into his background, Sam called it quits. Tomorrow would be a big day for her, and he didn't want to be the one yawning. She'd be seeing Silver Lake in the daylight and would hopefully like what she saw.

LEXI JERKED AWAKE and clutched the teal spread to her chest. Her heart pounded, flooding her body with adrenaline. It had been a dream—yes, only a dream. In it, Justin Kapok had entered her bedroom and was sticking her with a needle to sedate her. The part that scared the shit out of her the most was that she hadn't even been able to fight back.

When she focused on the cream-colored walls and the plush beige carpet, along with the shiny new deadbolt on the door, it helped to calm her down. She was safe, and best of all, Justin wasn't there to harm her. Normally, locking a bedroom door was overkill, but for a person on the run, it was a godsend.

Inhaling deeply to control her breathing, she finally calmed down. Because this room was underground, there were no windows, but the closed, green striped drapes helped give the illusion of being able to look outside. She leaned over and clicked on the light next to the bed. The clock read 9:35 a.m. Lexi was normally an early riser, but the long drive and constant worry had exhausted her. With no light entering the room to wake her, she'd overslept.

Planting her feet on the ground, she rose and a wave of dizziness assaulted her. She needed coffee and then a good breakfast.

Oh, crap. She didn't have any money to buy food. Maybe Sam would be willing to lend her some, or rather give her an advance on her new job—a job she really did need.

Lexi slipped into her jeans and a nicer shirt than she'd worn last night then grabbed her jacket before heading upstairs. The rich aroma of coffee teased her nose as she stepped into the main room. A blanket was tossed on the back of the sofa now, where there hadn't been one, before. Had Sam slept in the office last night? Given his protective nature, she wouldn't be surprised.

"Good morning," he said. "Coffee?"

"Yes, please. Black." She settled down at the same table where she'd had pizza last night.

"Sleep well?" he asked as he delivered the fresh brew.

"Yes." The sunlight pouring in through high windows brightened her mood.

"Connor called this morning and said his brother Devon would be heading up to Vermont to check on Justin Kapok."

A quick shot of adrenaline woke her up. Then guilt assaulted her. She'd be working for years if she had to pay them back. Flights and time were expensive. "He doesn't have to do that. As you might guess, I don't have that kind of money."

"We're in the protection business. We do a lot of pro bono work."

She swept a hand around. "Someone has to pay for this."

He smiled. "We have enough clients who do pay."

The rich aroma distracted her. She needed her caffeine fix in order to function, so Lexi sipped her coffee, and her muscles began to unwind. "So when do I start work?"

"We're closed today, but I can show you the ropes. How about we start after breakfast?"

As much as she didn't want to fall for this man, he was doing a good job of meeting her every need. "Perfect."

"Finish your coffee, and then I'll take you to the best little breakfast place in Silver Lake."

Never in her dreams did she think she'd be taken to breakfast the day after leaving Vermont. For now, she'd enjoy herself and later on, question why this was happening. At least with Sam by her side, she didn't have to worry about Justin.

She'd been told there were gods and goddesses in the shifter realm. Perhaps there were Wendayan deities too, one of whom might have been assigned to be her guardian angel.

"You're smiling," Sam said. "Care to share?"

Heat raced up her face. "Just being thankful for my temporary respite from the evil man." Bill was just as bad, or should she say just as weak, but he wouldn't care enough to come after her.

As soon as she said the word *temporary*, Sam's expression darkened. What was that about? He didn't even know her.

"Ready?"

"Yes."

She pushed back her chair and stood. Sam opened up the front door to exit the building, and the sun nearly blinded her. The sky was a cerulean blue with scattered white puffy clouds, and the ground was coated in pure whiteness. "It's beautiful," she said.

Sam inhaled deeply. "It looks like it snowed quite a lot last night. It smells fresh."

Maybe it was the fear that had resided in her for hours, or the relief of not having to be on the run for a while, but Lexi felt like a kid again—free and almost giddy. She stooped down, grabbed a handful of snow, and packed it tight. As if guided by an invisible hand, she stepped back a few feet and threw the cold projectile at him.

When she saw his eyes widen, she realized her mistake. Her pent up anxiety had caused her to toss it too hard, and it smacked him in the chest with enough force to elicit a grunt.

She rushed up to him. "I'm so sorry. I didn't mean to bean you that hard."

"Uh-huh. This is war, lady." The levity in his voice helped loosen the swirling in her belly.

He bent down and grabbed a handful of snow. Instead of making it into a ball, he rushed toward her and quickly dumped a bit of snow down her back.

"Arggh, that's cold." Her voice came out shrill.

"Serves you right." Sam winked.

He would pay for that. Lexi darted to the far side of his truck while Sam headed for a three-foot tall cement wall that bordered a retention pond and ducked behind it. Clearly, he understood what would happen next. She rolled five snowballs and placed them on the truck's hood for rapid firing. Sam did the same.

"I was a Marine, you know," he called from about fifteen feet away. "I've defused bombs and never had an accident. You aren't going to win, so you might as well give up now."

She laughed. "Is that so? You haven't seen my power and accuracy."

"Show me, fighter girl."

She'd never met a man so serious one minute and whimsical the next. Lexi might be strong and agile, but she wasn't fast enough to sneak up on him without him noticing. Having all of her projectiles within reach, she stepped out from behind the truck. "Show yourself; unless you're too scared?"

"Me? Scared?" Sam stood and immediately lobbed a snowball that fell at her feet, well short of its target.

"That all you got, cowboy?" She threw a fastball, but Sam managed to duck at the last second. It landed behind him.

"Is that how you want to play?" he asked, faking a scowl.

His next toss missed her head by inches, but that was only because she'd leaned to the side in order to throw her snowball. Wanting to win this battle, Lexi threw three snowballs in rapid succession. When the last one hit his arm and then burst into snowflakes, she raised her arms in victory. The goddess of humility must have been watching because Sam's snowball hit her square in the forehead a second later. She shrieked.

He came running. "Are you okay? I wasn't trying to hit you, I swear."

Lexi couldn't help but chuckle at the dismay on his face. "Other than being a bit embarrassed that you bested me, I'm fine." She swiped the water dripping down her forehead.

"You missed a spot." Sam moved close and when he dragged a thumb across her cheek, sparks burst off her body. Had she not been covered from head to toe, he'd have noticed her inappropriate response.

She stepped back. A moment later, her teeth returned to their human state. "Ah, thanks."

He smiled and wagged a finger. "While I admire your grit, be careful who you start a fight with. Definitely make certain not to engage with a man named Dalton Garner or his sister Jillian. They both move faster than the eye can track. Dalton's mate is almost as fast too."

She'd love to see that. "I'll be sure not to engage in a snowball fight with them."

"Smart woman, now hop in the truck. I'm starving," he said.

He was starving? She'd been the one who'd nose dived into a dumpster last night. Happier than she'd been in a long time, Lexi slid into the passenger's seat. "Do you normally sleep at the office?" she asked.

"First time."

Her pulse spiked. "Did you think Justin would come after me?"

He jammed the key in the ignition and fired up the engine. "No. As I said, this building is safe. We have security cameras around the perimeter, and the only way to get in requires a scan."

"Then why stay?" Lexi shouldn't have asked since his answer would only make him more attractive. Not only that, she was already fighting with her wolf too much. Sitting this close to him made her nails elongate and a few bones crack, threatening a shift. Using her strength and willpower, she forced them back.

"I didn't want you to need something in the middle of the night and find the place empty. Safe or not, when you're alone in a strange place, it can be scary."

Did he speak from experience? Had he woken up in some hellhole and been alone? As much as she wanted to know the answer, learning too much about him would make it harder to leave when the time came. "Thank you."

He glanced over at her and smiled, causing her body to nearly swoon.

*You can't leave now. He's your mate,* her wolf reminded her.

*Just watch me,* she shot back. *If Sam is my mate, I don't want trouble to find him too.*

*That's a lame excuse,* her wolf responded. *You're just scared.*

*Maybe I am. Now butt out.*

A phone rang and she automatically looked for her purse, only to remember she'd had no reason to bring it. She wasn't about to use any traceable credit cards either. Sam pressed a button on the dash. "What's up?"

"I contacted my brother, and Devon said he'd catch an afternoon flight to Vermont."

Her heart nearly stopped. What was this man planning to do? Tell Justin where she was? Or confront him? Neither scenario would end well.

"That's great. I appreciate it. Keep me posted," Sam said.

"Will do. Watch over Lexi, and tell her this will be over soon."

"I will." Sam disconnected and glanced over at her. "You okay with us butting into your affairs?"

# Chapter Four

AFTER LEARNING HOW aggressive Lexi was, he and Connor should have asked her permission first, before interfering in her life, but it was too late now; Devon was already on his way to Vermont.

"Depends on what this Devon person plans to do. Will he approach Justin?" she asked.

Clearly, she had no idea what he and his company did. "No. Devon will be gathering information on the side, trying to find out what Kapok is up to. If your stalker is planning to come after you, we'll know about it in advance." Her eyes lit up, making him want to do nice things for her every day just to see that expression.

"Really? That's awesome. I'll never be able to thank you."

*Being willing to stay here will be thanks enough.* Not voicing his thoughts, Sam continued to head down Maple Avenue toward the Silver Lake Café, hoping it wasn't too busy on a Sunday morning. Between church not letting out for another half hour and the fresh snowfall, he figured the place wouldn't be packed.

Wanting Lexi to have a good sense of the town, Sam pointed to the restaurant with the red awning. "There's Nate's Pizzeria where Connor picked up the food from last night."

"That pizza was fantastic. I'll be stopping by there in the future."

The word *future* had a nice ring to it. "Have you contacted your brother to let him know you're okay?" She seemed smart about not using credit cards, but was she willing to cut off all communications?

"No. I didn't want anyone to be able to trace my phone. Or is that an old wives' tale perpetuated by the movie industry?"

He liked her quick mind. "No, phones can be traced. It takes some equipment and some know-how to do it, but you were smart not to call." McKinnon and Associates had a burner phone, but he'd wait until he heard back from Devon before offering it to her. Her brother might convince her to return home, claiming he could protect her. For many reasons, Sam was against that idea.

"I can't email either." She slumped down in her seat, and Sam ached for her. He'd been in a few situations overseas where their communication devices had been down, and that really sucked. For the first month after he returned from that war torn zone, he'd had dreams of bombs going off and then learning that his communication devices were down, preventing him from warning his team to keep back.

"Just lay low for a few more days. Once we gather some intel, we'll know how to proceed."

"I can't tell you how much I appreciate this. I can never repay you."

*Oh, yes you can.* "Staying safe is payment enough."

Sam understood that he'd have to take it slow between them. Even though Lexi had shown she was capable of letting go of her worries for a short while—like when she'd tossed that snowball at him—fear still resided in her eyes. Until Justin Kapok was caught, Sam wouldn't put any pressure on her.

*What if she comes onto me?* If they truly were mates, her body would be going crazy with need. Then again, the recent events of the past might be so overwhelming that her mind might not be capable of thinking along those lines.

It was also possible he'd misread the signs about her being his mate. His inability to do mind control on her might have been a fluke. A horn honked, and Sam tapped his brakes.

He might not be in the service any longer, but he was still a soldier at heart and should be capable of staying on task regardless of what was happening around him. *Right.* Just being with Lexi distracted him.

"Here we are," he said with as much cheer as he could muster. He had to park three blocks from the restaurant. "Church is still in session, which means they've taken up every available space." He nodded to the building across the street.

"That's okay. Since the wind isn't blowing, I'd rather walk anyway. The suite is beautiful, but it can be a bit claustrophobic at times. I'm a true lover of light and the outdoors."

"I understand, but having no windows in a safe place is a necessary evil." He jumped out of his truck and rushed over to her side. Before he could open her door, Lexi had already slipped out, clearly not used to chivalry. "Watch your step. Ice can form under the snow."

She laughed. "Remember, I'm from Vermont. I'm used to this stuff."

He hadn't been thinking, and that was a first for him. Lexi must be emitting some kind of blocking signal that prevented all rational thought.

Once they reached the restaurant, Sam managed to open the door before Lexi could reach the wooden handle. Inside, noise filled the small space. Surprisingly, the café was fairly packed. Damn. He hoped they didn't have a long wait. While he had a ton of questions he wanted to ask her, Sam decided it might be better to let her lead the discussion since she had no real reason to trust him yet.

Tangie Anderson, the hostess, smiled up at him from her podium. She'd asked him out numerous times, but Sam had always turned her down, stating he was in the middle of a case and didn't have time. The last thing he needed right now was for one of his sister's friends to flirt with him or make a scene.

Wanting to show Tangie that he and Lexi were together, he placed a hand on Lexi's back. "Table for two."

The light in Tangie's eyes dimmed. She then checked the paper on her stand. "Sure, follow me."

She led them to a booth in the back, which was perfect for having a private conversation. He motioned that Lexi slide in first and then he sat across from her.

"Connie will be your server." Tangie spun around and headed back, wiggling her hips, probably hoping to entice him. Poor woman didn't stand a chance.

"I need to confess something," Lexi said, looking off to the side.

His chest tightened, immediately thinking she might have made up some detail in her story. Hopefully that wasn't the case, especially since several of Connor's men were working to help her. "About what?"

"My last name isn't Daniels. That was my mom's maiden name. My real name is Lexi Laramie."

He repeated her name in his head, liking the way it rolled off his tongue. "Okay. I'll let Connor know. Anything else?"

"No."

Asking her why she lied wasn't necessary. If he'd been in her shoes, he might not have told the truth right away either. She'd come clean possibly because she trusted him, and that made his chest swell with pride.

Their server came over and they both ordered coffee. "So what do you do when you're not saving runaway women?" she asked, seemingly relieved at having cleared the air.

Sam laughed at her description of him. "As I mentioned, I was in the service. I returned to Silver Lake less than a year ago, and I'm still trying to adjust to civilian life. When Connor learned of my talent, he offered me a job, and I've been trying to hone my craft ever since."

"Connor sounds like a great guy. He gave you a chance, and now, he's helping me too."

Sam was pleased she understood how close people were in this town. "He is."

"If you work all the time, what do you do for fun?"

To be honest, Sam was a bit surprised she wanted to learn anything about him, especially since her goal was to leave town as soon as possible. He suspected that she was just making small talk, but he was happy to tell her anything she wanted to know. "I enjoy physical activities. In the summer months I run, and in winter I like to snowboard. Growing up, I hiked all the time."

Her eyes widened. "Hmm. I pictured you as the type to be at the rifle range every weekend, even when you were still in school and had to study."

He laughed at her image of him. "I won't deny I spent time practicing those skills, but I was a bit reckless until I enlisted. Hell, my buddies and I did crap that was way too dangerous. Back then, I thought I was invincible."

She smiled. "That sounds like Ronan."

"Ronan?"

"My brother. He's three years older than me and is fearless—or rather he was fearless when we were growing up. Now, he's a lot more cautious."

From the way she spoke of her brother, she was very fond of him. "What does he do for a living?"

"He's a bounty hunter."

Sam refrained from showing any enthusiasm, but inside he was thrilled. It meant Lexi would understand if he had to be called out in the middle of the night on some assignment—not that she'd be staying he reminded himself. Men like her brother put their lives on the line every day, just like Sam.

"Excellent. Has he ever been able to use his wolf to take down a perpetrator?" Sam made sure to keep his voice low to prevent anyone from overhearing.

Her brows furrowed, and she glanced to the side. "I have no idea. I don't think it's something he would tell me. He thinks I'd worry too much, which I would. Even though our Clan isn't very large, we want to make sure we aren't found out. So far, the townsfolk are blissfully unaware of werewolves."

"Our residents don't know that wolves, bears, or tigers exist either."

She mouthed *wolves* and *bears* and *tigers*. "Oh, my!"

He chuckled. "I can see I have to bring you up to speed." Sam leaned forward and, once more, made sure to keep his voice low. "Connor is a wolf, but Jackson, another member of our team, is a bear. His brother's partner in the sheriff's department is a tiger. Kip, the last member of the team is a Wendayan. Kip and I are the only two who aren't shifters. We both have unique talents that help us foil the bad guys however."

Just then the server returned with their coffees. "Have you two decided?"

Sam planned to order his usual, but he motioned Lexi to go first.

"Two eggs over easy, two strips of bacon, and an English muffin please," she said.

The server jotted it down. "For you Sam?"

"My usual."

Connie nodded and headed back to the kitchen. "If you eat here a lot," Lexi said, "how do you stay so fit?"

He patted his stomach. "That's sweet of you to say." In reality, he was thrilled she noticed. "I like to work out. I think I mentioned that Connor's father built a gym in the basement so we could stay fit. Part of the space is for sparring and is large enough to accommodate the shifters to exercise their animals as well."

"That is impressive."

"When we have to fight the Changelings, it's often in animal form for those that can shift."

She held up her hands then glanced around. "Changelings?"

"Shh."

"Sorry."

"When we're back at the office, I'll tell you about them."

"I can't wait."

Sam appreciated her enthusiasm.

Their meal arrived and they both dug in. He liked that Lexi had a good appetite. Too many women worried about their weight, but not her. Lexi was perfect.

"Mmm, this is so good." She moaned, and just like that his cock hardened.

Sam's thoughts turned to what sounds she'd make in the throes of passion, and thankfully, he was able to control his blue sparks.

Not wanting to discuss shifters any more, he changed the subject. "Have you ever been snowmobiling?"

Her eyes widened once more. "Not since I was a kid. One of my friend's dad used to take both of us into the hills on the weekends. We always had a blast."

Sam bet they'd have a better time. If he could show her what Silver Lake had to offer, she might reconsider her dream of walking on the Florida beaches.

He pulled out his phone. "Let me see if I can borrow one. The day is too perfect not to spend it outside."

"I thought you wanted to show me the ropes, so to speak."

She really seemed intent on doing a good job. "We can do that later."

Lexi sipped her coffee, looking over the rim of her cup. "Are you spending all this time with me so I won't be alone, or because you're trying to take my mind off of my stalker?"

Sam winked at her. "How about if I just want to cut loose and have a carefree day? My sister and parents are always complaining that all I do is work."

Lexi smiled and hope filled him. "Then I say we have a blast while we can."

SAM WAS RIGHT. Spending the day outside helped take her mind off Justin, but snuggling behind the hunky man caused a whole different set of problems. For starters, blue sparks kept flying everywhere, especially when he'd take a corner a bit too fast, and she had to clutch him tight. Twice her scalp had itched, a precursor to shifting. Had she not been wearing gloves, he might have noticed how her hands had begun to change.

Everything about Sam appealed to her, but eventually he'd end up like so many of the men in her Clan. They would profess to have found their mate, yet within a few years, they would take up with a different human woman. Some had gone through several ladies, and yet these humans never seemed to catch on to what these shifter men were capable of. They just liked what they had to offer.

Her mom claimed this whole fated mate thing was true. Just look at her and Dad, she'd say. In reality, it was a bunch of bullshit. Lexi just wished her wolf would shut up about Sam being her mate and remember all the times she'd been misled by a man. She was the one who was interested in him, not the other way around. His sparks didn't seem to be shooting off him like they were on her.

Sam suddenly maneuvered the huge machine up a steep slope. "Hang on," he called back to her.

He didn't need to worry; her grip was already super tight. Having her chest plastered against his back caused her imagination to go wild. She might not be able to feel the contours of his body with all the material between them, but she could imagine what it would be like to press her breasts against his naked skin.

*Mate*, her wolf chimed in.

Geesh, *Shut up already. It's bad enough I have to be so close to him. I don't need you spouting lies.* Or was it the truth?

The snowmobile jumped over a small hill, jarring her out of her reverie. She shouldn't be thinking about Sam in that way. He slowed as he neared the crest, and she lifted her head to see the vista. The snow in the distance sparkled, and the air was still. The snow under them, however, was spraying in every direction, making a pretty vision.

When they reached the top, Sam stopped and cut the engine. Her head still buzzed, and her body vibrated. Lexi couldn't remember feeling more alive. Sam tapped her leg and she eased off then removed her helmet. The air was cold on her face and ears, but it was refreshing at the same time after the long ride.

Sam took off his helmet and grabbed her hand. "You've got to see this view."

Heart racing from the whole exhilarating experience, she went with the flow and had to take long steps to keep up with him. For once in her life, she told her analytic side to shove it. She was here in Silver Lake for only a short time, and she wanted to enjoy it.

He led her over to where the snow covered trees ended and then pointed to a small area below. "See that empty space to the east?"

"Where the trees just seem to stop?"

"Yes. That's Silver Lake."

Part of her wished she could see it in the summer. She bet it would be beautiful. "I guess the town should have a lake if it was named after one."

Sam smiled. "Indeed." He retrieved the backpack from the compartment under the seat. "There's a small cave down a ways where we can have our picnic."

"There's a cave, as in a place where bats live?"

He laughed. "I never thought you'd be afraid of a blind bat."

"I'm not…okay maybe a little. They kind of creep me out when I'm in my human form."

"Then I guess I'll just have to protect you if they attack."

Lexi shivered, despite believing he would. She followed Sam for about six hundred feet along the ridge. "I feel like I'm in heaven up here," she said, looking all around. Being so high up made her believe no one could harm her.

"I feel the same way."

When they reached the outcroppings, Sam stepped through a three-foot wide slit in the rocks, and she followed right behind him. The moment she entered the cave, the outside noises ceased to exist. The only sounds were their footsteps echoing off the stone walls.

"I didn't expect it to be so much warmer in here." She guessed there was about twenty degrees difference from when they'd been out in the open.

He turned halfway around. "That's why I picked it. The rocks block the wind."

She wished she could have seen the color of his eyes to judge his mood, but there was barely enough light to see her feet. At least she had her shifter sight, which made her wonder how Sam didn't trip.

Maneuvering around a few rocks, he reached the back wall where a small fire ring existed. Next to the ring sat some firewood. "Did you do this?" she asked, nodding to the wood.

"No. A lot of people use this cave if they spend the night around here. Most of the time there's leftover wood."

"Cool. Do we need to put a Do Not Disturb sign on the outside or something?" He cleared his throat, acting as if he thought she was considering making love. It wasn't a stupid idea. The hot fire would make it possible. Obviously, he wasn't thinking along those lines. "I was kidding," she said.

Not completely. She wanted to have Sam to herself even if it was just for a picnic. She wouldn't appreciate other hikers barging in on them.

"I think our snowmobile and footprints are enough to keep other humans away."

And other shifters hopefully. "Good point."

From the backpack, he pulled out a small packet, maybe three inches long by one inch high. He ripped it open with his teeth, and then shook out a four-foot by six-foot emergency blanket made from a silvery reflective material.

"This will keep us dry. Have a seat," Sam said.

While Lexi had been on a few picnics, never had any of them been in a cave in winter. When she dropped down, she was delighted not to have a cold butt. "This blanket really works."

"I know," Sam said. "We used them in the service, but only if we were in the high desert where it grew cold at night.

He emptied the backpack. Before they went on their excursion, they'd stopped at the store to pick up the picnic supplies. Sam had been amazing, trying hard to figure out what she liked to eat. They'd both agreed on fried chicken, potato salad, and potato chips, though she doubted Sam ate like this very often.

He handed her a bottle of water then held up his. "To a beautiful day."

She smiled and tapped her bottle against his. "Indeed. So, tell me about these Changelings."

# Chapter Five

S AM EXPLAINED HOW these Changelings came to be, and what havoc they'd caused in Silver Lake. Lexi had no idea that such mutant creatures existed. "As horrible as they sound," she said, "they seem to have a few similarities to some of the people in my Clan."

"Like Justin?"

At his name, worry rushed in. "Yes, like him, as well as many others."

"Why do you say that? Do you think some of your clansmen might have tainted genes?"

She hadn't planned to discuss her Clan members' infidelity, but she wanted him to understand where she stood in regards to shifters. "Not that I've heard of, but lately it appears that my Clan members have grown discontent. Many of the shifter matings have ended in divorce, or the equivalent of it in the shifter world. To me, it's possible there is something genetically wrong with some of them, because I've been told that when two shifters mated, it was for life."

"That's what Connor told me too. I thought all shifters around the world were the same—other than the Changelings."

"Apparently, not."

Okay, she never should have brought up that depressing topic, and she needed to change the subject. She considered asking about his time in the service, but most likely what he did was still classified. One of her brother's friends had served, but when he returned, his PTSD was so debilitating that he had to seek counseling. War really messed with a person's head. Sam, thankfully, seemed to have returned unscathed—or else he hid his issues well.

"Why did you decide to leave the service? You are still young."

"I thought I could do more good at home. Besides, I missed my family, though my parents are still on a sabbatical for another year."

He'd mentioned he had a sister, but he hadn't spoken of his folks. "Do they work at a University?"

"Not exactly, though they do teach. They work at a spiritual camp that caters to psychics and such."

"Really? That's cool."

"I guess." He gnawed on the last chicken leg. "My sister, Teagan, benefitted the most from it, but I never felt as if I fit in with all that creative stuff. Sure I have my abilities, but I like regimen, being on time, and thoroughly examining a topic. My folks however, don't seem to notice that time exists. They're happy, so maybe their lifestyle is better."

"I like organization and order too. I guess I don't want to leave the future to chance."

He dropped the bare chicken leg he'd eaten in the trash bag. "It must have taken a lot of guts for you to leave your hometown then."

She nodded. "It was, but I had to if I valued my life. While I can fight one wolf, I'm not ready to take on Justin and his team of followers." Talking about her stalker caused her mood to plummet once more.

Sam reached over and squeezed her hand. "You don't have to worry about him here. My team will make sure you stay safe."

There were those wonderful words again. Sam must have sensed the change in her mood, because he kept quiet and began to pack up their food. Lexi helped.

Once they finished, Sam rolled up their thin blanket, stuffed it into the sack, and led her back outside. The bright sun made her squint, but the fresh air helped reinvigorate her. Halfway back to their snowmobile, Sam faced her. "Have you ever slid down a hill on your butt?"

She laughed. "Nope. I've used skis, a sled, a flying saucer, and a snowboard, but never my rear."

"I know just the place."

For someone who liked order and regimen, Sam sure was spontaneous. Perhaps all those years in the service had worn on him, and this was his chance to let go.

At the snowmobile, he set the backpack on the seat. "It's just over this ridge," Sam said. "Come on."

"I can't wait."

Together, they plowed through the snow. From the workout, her body began to heat, and she was so tempted to shift and romp around. That chance at freedom however would require her to undress if she wanted to have something to wear on the ride back to town. Not only would it be chilly, she wasn't sure she could keep her naked form from Sam's sight when she shifted back. Tempting fate wasn't her thing, so in the end, she decided to just enjoy being human.

When they moved past a grove of pines, he pointed to a treeless slope. "How about here?" he asked.

"You want to show me how to do this?"

"There's not much to it. Just sit down, lift your legs, and push off."

That seemed easy enough. Because she was so much lighter than Sam, and her pants were nylon, she bet she'd have less friction. That translated into moving faster. "I'll race you."

He laughed. "You are so going down."

"Not unless you have a turbo booster shooting out your butt." The second she said it, Lexi regretted her crassness, but hey, she always spoke her mind.

"You're on. What's the prize?"

She was about to suggest that the loser had to kiss the winner, but that would only land her in trouble. "The loser buys hot chocolate with marshmallows and whipped cream."

"Oh, that is definitely a deal."

Once they were in position, Sam nodded. "Ready, set, go," he shouted.

Lexi lifted her legs and pushed off. The hill was steep enough that she slid fast at first until the snow built up between her legs. Then she came to a stop. Crap. After digging her way out, she started again.

Sam seemed to be experiencing the same issue, but somehow he managed to be a few feet ahead of her. Dang. Lexi hated losing. When the slope began to level off, she needed to change her tactics. She lifted her legs higher and leaned back, lessening the amount of contact with the ground. For the last few yards, she dipped her hands into the snow and paddled. Neck in neck with Sam, she dug in harder and faster. While there wasn't a definitive end point, where the ground leveled out seemed to be a good ending spot.

Just as she slowed to a stop, Sam slid next to her. Lexi dropped back and lowered her legs, giving her abs a break.

"You won!" he said. "Great job."

Exhilarated, she let out a sigh. He dropped onto his back too, his breath coming out a bit labored. "I don't know when I've had so much fun," she said. The clouds floated overhead, contrasting with the bright blue sky. Everything was perfect.

"Me neither. I need to do this more often." He sounded wistful, as if he spent all of his time working.

Lexi rolled onto her side and lifted up on her elbow. Her butt was wet, but she didn't care. Adrenaline was coursing through her system from the race, erasing every bad thought in her head.

*Kiss him*, her wolf urged. *Just to thank him for what he's done.*

For once she didn't balk. She owed this man a lot. Without giving it a second thought, Lexi leaned forward and cupped his cheek. "Thank you for today."

Before he had the chance to respond or stop her, she closed her eyes and kissed him. In seconds, her whole body turned traitor, sending erotic pulses straight to her core. Her eyes had probably already turned amber. She opened them, only to find Sam had shut his, and his moan made her forget all of the reasons why she should stop.

He wrapped one hand around her neck while placing the other along the side of her face. When he teased open her lips, she could no more turn him down than she could have stayed another minute in her dad's trailer.

The first taste had her heart rate ramping up and her body heating. Her sparks flew so much that she literally pulsed waves of blue. Holy shit, Batman. That had never happened before.

*Mate, mate*, her wolf chanted.

Who cares who or what he was. Right now, she couldn't get enough of him as his fresh scent imprinted itself on her brain. Moving closer, she fully pressed up against him, and her bones cracked. When the bulge in his pants became evident, the rational part of herself jerked her back to reality.

Lexi broke the kiss. "Sorry, I got a little carried away."

Sam grinned, and dimples creased his cheeks. "I liked it a lot."

As if the gods were on her side once more, a large dark cloud blocked the sun, forcing her to look up. "Do you think another storm is coming?"

That was a dumb thing to say, but if she didn't talk about something other than her intense reaction, she'd probably lean in and kiss him again, and she wasn't sure she had the willpower to stop a second time.

"It's hard to say, but mountain weather can be fickle. Are you saying you want to head back?" he asked, his voice tinged with disappointment.

*No. I want to stay here with you like this forever.* "Sure."

He stood and helped her to her feet. It was better this way. She'd gotten the urge to taste him out of the way, and the last thing she needed was to become distracted by Sam Pompley. No matter what Sam said about having someone keep an eye on Justin, the man was capable of finding her. Justin had what seemed like an endless supply of money at his fingertips—illegally procured she was sure. He was the type to hop on a private jet and fly down to Tennessee should he learn of her location. Having fun with Sam like this could not only cost her to lose her life, but it could also put others in danger.

When they reached the snowmobile, Sam dangled the keys from his finger. "Do you want to give it a try?"

"Me?" Her pulse raced. She hadn't driven one since she'd turned nineteen.

"If you don't feel comfortable, I—"

She snatched them from his hand. "No! I'm good."

Lexi slapped her helmet on, excited to take control. Sam stored the backpack and then donned his headgear. He looked really cute in it too. She climbed on and he slid behind her. Only then did she realize what being the driver meant. He was free to hold her as tightly as he wished. His legs would be pressed against her thighs, his chest to her back, and his crotch would be pressed against—*don't even go there.*

If they didn't have to wear helmets, she could imagine him nibbling on her ear as she made her way down the hill, trying to distract her. Stupid wolf, putting ideas into her head. If she shifted in the middle of the ride, they'd crash for sure.

SAM HAD ASKED Lexi to drive for two reasons. One, he wanted her to experience some control over her life. Victims often mentioned how helpless they felt. Lexi was right to leave the abusive situation, but without any financial support and an unknown future, she had to be scared.

Perhaps, the biggest reason for asking her to drive was that having her arms around him had almost caused him to lose control once or twice. With her pressed against his back, Sam's mind had wandered into dangerous territory. Being wrapped around her wasn't going to be any better, but what a ride it would be. He longed to see if what they were experiencing right now could be everlasting. Sure, she said she wanted to head on down to Florida, but if they could figure out a way to convince Justin to leave her alone, Sam and Lexi might have a future together.

He'd always believed he'd end up with an ambitious woman who yearned to take control of her life, and Lexi had those traits in spades. She also had a deep love of life. For the next few minutes, his goal was to convince her to let go and enjoy herself.

Sam inwardly chuckled. Hadn't his parents said the same thing to him? Maybe he and Lexi were alike.

"You ready?" she asked.

"Take us home."

Sam merely grabbed her waist instead of entombing her in his embrace. He didn't want to scare her or constrict her so much that she couldn't steer. As he anticipated, she drove cautiously as she headed down the mountainside. While careful, she handled the big machine well, adeptly maneuvering around clumps of trees. When they reached the small field near the road, Sam was disappointed their outing had come to an end, but at least that kiss would stay with him for a long time.

Instead of cutting the engine, Lexi gunned it, sending sprays of snow everywhere. The first turn had him holding on tight and laughing. She let out a whoop as she drove even faster, pushing the machine to the max. A left turn followed by a right almost threw him, but he pressed his thighs tighter against the seat and moved in unison with her sensuous body.

Just as quickly as the little exhibition began, she returned to the road and stopped. Adrenaline soared through his system. Never had he expected her to respond that way. To think she'd been so skittish when he and Connor had found her. Having her kiss him a day later blew his mind. Letting Lexi take the lead—at least until she was more comfortable about him—had been for the best.

She tapped his leg, and he dismounted. His legs were even a bit shaky. "You did well!" he said.

She slipped off her helmet and smiled. "Thanks. It was easy to handle."

"I could tell. You ready for your first day of real training?" he asked. While it wouldn't take much to teach someone as sharp as Lexi how to handle customers, he needed to discuss what each man brought to the job. He also would like to complete her education about the Changelings and explain a little more about what they were capable of. After that, he'd offer her some physical training to help with self-defense, something he was looking forward to—unless all that touching eroded his resolve to keep his distance.

# Chapter Six

THE SECURITY WORK at the McKinnon and Associates' branch in Pennsylvania was going well; so well in fact that taking time off to fly up to Vermont had forced Devon McKinnon to reassign some of his usual tasks to his trusted employees. He didn't hesitate to accept the job however, since his younger brother Connor had requested his help. Working with the team in Silver Lake always proved exciting.

Since arriving in Vermont, Devon had learned that Justin Kapok frequently visited the Bull's Head Bar on Mondays. It was ladies' night. Connor had forwarded a picture of Lexi's stalker to him, along with a few articles about the man and his habits. Apparently, much of Kapok's time was spent gambling at private homes. If Devon needed to gain access to one of these homes, it would take some creativity on his part, but he could do it.

From what his brother told him about the case, this man was totally immoral, though it was uncertain if he dealt in human trafficking or was merely a gambler with no conscience. Regardless, Kapok was after Lexi, and that meant Devon had to make sure he was aware of the man's whereabouts at all times.

Devon slid into an empty booth of the restaurant bar, keeping his gaze on the rest of the customers. Booths lined one wall and were parallel to a bar where almost every stool was occupied—mostly by men in jeans ranging in age from twenty to fifty. Between the booths and the bar sat eight more tables, three of which had at least one occupant. At the far end of the room was a small stage—empty right now—behind a ten-foot by fifteen-foot dance floor. A Kenny Chesney song was playing over the loud speaker, but no one was dancing.

Devon guessed the bathrooms were across from the stage, but from the way the room was configured, he didn't have a direct line of sight.

Even with his sensitive shifter hearing, the noise in the bar was tolerable, at least for now. Then again, it was still early.

A pretty blonde in a very skimpy waitress outfit bounced up to him. "What can I get you, cowboy?"

Devon was a lot of things, but cowboy wasn't one of them. Wanting good service, he refrained from correcting her. "Anything on draft." He winked to help boost the chance she might provide him with some information if needed.

"You got it, sugar. You from around here?"

Given her accent, she wasn't. "Just passing through."

Her shoulders sagged. "Too bad. One beer coming right up." While she maintained her smile, the corners of her lips sagged, as if she was hoping he'd be staying in town a while.

As unobtrusively as possible, Devon glanced around for his target but didn't find him. He wasn't worried though. According to several people he'd spoken to, Justin Kapok would be there tonight.

An hour later, five shifter signatures entered and approached the bar. One of the men was Kapok. At least now Devon could report that he hadn't left in search of Lexi.

A few seconds later, five bar seats suddenly vacated, and Devon couldn't help but wonder what Justin had said to them. On the other hand, his reputation might have preceded him. Once seated, all five men ordered drinks and his entourage laughed at something Justin said. From everyone's cheery attitudes, the man didn't seem to be sulking over losing Lexi.

Tomorrow, he'd check out Lexi's dad to make sure Kapok hadn't left him for dead or outright killed him.

After polishing off his beer, Devon texted Connor to say Lexi was safe for another day. Because Devon pretended that the weight of the world had landed on his shoulders, no one other than the waitress seemed to pay him any mind. Perfect.

Devon was about to call it a night when the main door open and his body suddenly went crazy with need. What the hell? The hairs on the back of his hands sprouted, forcing him to place them on his lap. This wasn't good.

As much as he didn't want to glance around, he couldn't help it. When he spotted the glorious woman, his chest squeezed tight at her beauty. Devon had seen many women in his days—and had slept with a fair number of those—but this woman defied description. She had to be a good five feet ten inches, and her long, wavy dark auburn hair coupled with those mile-long legs made her even more spectacular. From the confident sway of her walk, he bet she'd be a hellion to deal with.

A wave of disgust washed over him at his unprofessional behavior. Devon was here to find out what Justin Kapok planned to do, not have the best sex of his life. If he botched this assignment, not only would his younger brother be pissed, his older brother Rye and their dad would be furious too.

When the woman strutted by Justin and his men, one by one every head turned. Devon didn't have to imagine what was going through their minds. Justin held up his hand and slid off his stool. His posse remained. Interesting.

Without looking back, the woman strolled, or rather floated, to the dance floor, where now three other couples were doing a slow dance. Her nearly see-through top made her appear ghostlike, yet highly provocative. As if she knew Justin would follow, she spun around and crooked her finger for him to dance with her.

All Devon could see was Kapok's back, but the woman smiled when he drew her close to his chest and held on tight. Something ugly dug into Devon's stomach, but he tried to tamp it down. This was a business trip with no room for pleasure.

What he wouldn't give to hear what those two were talking about. Sex, most likely, and would it be her place or his? Kapok's four tag-alongs seemed to have lost interest in the pair and began chatting. It certainly didn't look as if they were plotting a way to capture Lexi.

The waitress seemed to have taken pity on him and brought him over some bread. "You looked hungry," she said.

Devon hadn't thought about food, but once he smelled the fresh loaf, his stomach grumbled. "Thanks. How about a hamburger?"

"You got it, handsome. And another beer?"

"I'm good." While he rarely got a buzz from drinking, he needed to stay sharp. Besides, he was hatching a plan.

While he waited for the food, he nibbled on the bread. Kapok danced with the woman for one more song then escorted her back to the bar. The man who had been sitting next to Justin offered her his seat, though Devon doubted it was out of chivalry. His boss would demand it.

No sooner had she sat down than Devon's meal arrived. He ate half of his hamburger then grabbed his empty glass. After sliding out of his booth, he strode up to the bar, positioning himself between the man at the end and a young woman who was talking with another friend. Devon waved his glass at the bartender. Waiting for the refill he didn't intend to drink, he listened to the conversation.

"So it's a deal?" the woman said to Kapok.

"Hey, as long as I get the girl, you can do what you want."

The girl? Did that mean Lexi? Devon's pulse jumped. The woman leaned over and kissed his cheek. "I'll see you tomorrow then."

As she turned, Kapok grabbed her arm, but the smile on her face never diminished. "Where are you going, sugar? We're just getting started."

"You couldn't handle me," she said plucking his fingers from her arm.

Devon nearly crushed his glass, ready to defend her honor should Kapok hurt her.

"What can I get you, buddy?" the bartender asked, pulling his attention away from the pair.

"Another draft."

"Sure thing." He filled up the glass and handed it back to him. "I'll tell Serena to add it to your tab."

"Thanks."

Devon returned to his booth, not liking how that conversation ended. One thing he did know was that it was going to be a long, sleepless night watching Justin Kapok.

AFTER SAM TOOK Lexi back, he escorted her into his office. She smiled when she spotted the three photos of military men. "Were these men in your unit?"

He turned toward the photo and his chest expanded, as if he were in their presence once more. "Yes. I like to think that I'm watching over them now."

"Were you always a protector?" She spun around to face him.

"My mom says I was. It seemed to have been bred into me."

How sweet was that? Lexi was surprised he hadn't been scooped up by some woman long ago. Then again, he had just returned from serving where he'd been focused on helping keep our country safe. "What did you want to show me?"

He lifted the lid to his laptop. "I want to show you the men who might be passing through here. Many people help us from time to time, and I want you to know them from the clientele."

"Excellent."

He pulled over a chair next to his desk chair and motioned she sit down. "Here's a pad of paper and a pen to jot down notes. It might get complicated," he said as he handed them to her.

She wished she'd taken the time to pick up her iPad before leaving Vermont, but she'd been in a hurry. "I'm ready."

Sam showed her pictures of Jackson Murdoch, who was a bear shifter, and Kip Landon, who was a Wendayan capable of creating electricity. "Both work here. Kip's talents extend to lock picking, but his main benefit is in cutting power to places."

"Wow."

"I'm impressed too. He's usually the auxiliary guy because he's not a shifter, but he has tasered a few wolves in his day. Kip's mate is Teagan, who is my sister. Kip also has a twin brother, Randy, who's a lawyer. While they are not identical, you might confuse them. Thankfully, we've not needed his services yet."

"And Jackson?"

"Jackson is our technical genius." He told her about their drone and how it had helped solve a few cases. "He can hack into anything and find dirt on a sterilized scalpel. Needless to say, he's a very valuable asset. His dad was one of the founders."

"Does he have a mate?"

"Yes. Her name is Ainsley. She is rare in that she can make herself invisible."

"Really? I know we Wendayans are talented, but I didn't know that was even possible." Lexi wanted to see that. "Now I'm even more impressed."

"While she's a wolf-Wendayan mix like you, she is a rare breed in that she can tell a regular shifter from a Changeling, and she can identify whether a shifter is a wolf, bear, or tiger."

"Never in my life did I imagine such a talented group of people existed in one spot."

"The whole town of Silver Lake is even more extraordinary. We have a man who is immortal, and he's married to the goddess Naliana."

She leaned back and studied him. "Are you making this shit up?"

Sam held up a palm. "I swear on the American flag that I'm telling the truth."

She'd heard of Naliana, the goddess who paired mates. "Okay. Continue. I'm ready to be wowed some more." She still believed he was pulling her leg. Sam then seemed to run through half the town. Between the Alpha, Beta, and the Beta's partner in the sheriff's department, her head swam. "I'm not sure I can keep track of everyone."

"You'll do fine. I'll make up a family tree for you. Connor has two older brothers and a younger sister and brother. The oldest, Rye is the Alpha of the Clan, and in between them is Devon. He's the one keeping tabs on Justin. The youngest brother, Finn, bartends at his uncle's bar, and his twin sister, Chelsea, is a vet tech."

"Got it." She had Ronan. That was all. Her father was now dead to her.

"I'm sure there will be some get together either this weekend or next. Once you see them face-to-face, it'll be easier to keep everyone straight." He stood. "You've seen where you'll be working. It's not well set up, but once you get settled, we can give you whatever you need." Sam pulled open the top desk drawer and fished out a phone. "This is a burner phone. It can't be traced, so call us on this. All of our numbers are programmed in here."

She was about to ask if she could call Ronan, but she'd wait until he finished showing her what to do. Instead of heading to the front as she expected, he led her down the hallway. Near the end, he opened a door by pressing his finger against the scanner.

"Will I need access too?" she asked.

"Yes. Jackson is in charge of that. He'll take your print and do whatever he does to make it work."

Lexi had never felt so welcomed anywhere she'd worked. When she'd taught school, the other teachers were too busy worrying about their own students to help guide her. She suspected that if Justin Kapok didn't exist, she could thrive here. The air slowly leaked out of her body at the thought of leaving Silver Lake though.

*Stay, stay,* her wolf urged. *Sam's the one for us.*

Lexi wouldn't mind indulging in some wild pleasures, but she had to make certain to steel her heart against believing everything he told her was true. Perfect men did not exist.

They entered a foyer that contained another staircase. "Where does this go?" she asked.

"To our workout room. I thought you might like to learn a few tricks."

She laughed. "I'm a wolf and you're…human."

"True, but there could be times when you'll have to fight in your human form. Mind you, I'd prefer you never leave this building, but I know that's not practical. Having fighting skills are always a good thing."

While she had strength on her side, her skills weren't developed. "Is there a shooting range down here too?" They had everything else. Not that she'd ever shot a gun in her life, but this was a security firm.

"No, but Silver Lake has a gun range that we can use."

"If I'm here for a while, I'd like to learn. Being able to defend myself might come in handy."

At the bottom of the steps, he pushed open a door that led to an area the size of the large room upstairs. One side contained gym equipment while the other half had mats on the floor.

"I'm not exactly dressed to lift weights," she said.

"We're not going there." Sam led her to the padded area. "I want to show you some self defense moves, though I hope you won't have to use them."

"I'm game." Not only did she have nothing else to do, if she could get in some more touches, her day would be perfect.

"What should you do if a man tries to attack you and you aren't in a place where you can shift?" Sam asked.

"Run?"

He laughed. "Running is good if you think you are faster than that person."

"I'm pretty fast, but I might not have the right shoes for sprinting." She tried to picture a dark alley or a crowded parking lot in which maneuvering would be difficult.

"Agreed. I'll show you some moves. Ready?"

"Yes."

"First, if you are attacked, go for the eyes like this. Surprise is the key." Sam curved his forefinger and middle finger and pretended to poke out her eyes. "If you think you're life is in danger, you have to take him down the quickest way you can."

She wasn't sure she could poke out someone's eyes, but if she were desperate enough, she might try. "That's pretty gruesome."

"I know, but if your life is on the line, you'll have to try it. If he blocks your arm when you are trying for his eyes, or if you can't reach him, you'll need a different tactic. If he strikes you, and you just stand there, he'll be able to knock you down."

He demonstrated slowly. The punch was light, but even that blow knocked her off balance, but she didn't tumble. "I can tell that a harder hit would be difficult to come back from," she said.

"Correct. So here's what you need to do to combat it. As I come toward you with my fist, turn to the side and see what happens."

Sam demonstrated again. When Lexi twisted, the blow glanced off her, and she didn't even need to adjust her balance. "That was cool."

"For you, yes, but not for the attacker, because he is now off balance. Every time you turn, squirm, duck, or whatever, it makes you *unavailable*. That means you're unavailable to be hit. Now here's what else you can do. As you turn, move closer to me and try to hit me."

In slow motion, Sam threw a punch. As his hand neared her body, she not only twisted, but she stepped forward, and her wolf panted from the closeness. Her scalp itched, and a few hairs began to poke out of her arms.

*Stop it*, she commanded her wolf.

*I can't help it.*

*Try.*

Ignoring her wolf's whimpers, Lexi did a slow motion punch to Sam's stomach. In real life, she would have aimed lower.

*Touch him down there*, her wolf said. *You can always say it was a mistake.*

Sam grabbed her hand, but not before she met with resistance. "That was awesome," she said, thrilled she'd made contact.

"When you attack back, it's called being *unavoidable*. Your goal then is to be unavailable and then unavoidable."

She smiled. "Let's try it again. Only this time move a bit faster."

He laughed. "You do know that no matter how good you become at combat, we aren't taking you out on assignment?"

She stuck out her tongue, enjoying the whole concept of just being herself again. "I know, but you can never have too much knowledge."

"Very true."

"Okay, go for it."

# Chapter Seven

S AM NEVER SHOULD have tried to teach Lexi how to fight because being this close to her was messing with his head. In the service, he'd taken many combat classes and eventually ended up teaching a few. Even when he taught females, he never had this kind of reaction. This was more proof that Lexi was his mate.

*Or am I being a wishful fool?* He might want her, but Lexi had made it clear she intended to leave just as soon as Kapok was neutralized. She'd either decide to return to Vermont to be with her brother and friends, or hightail it down to Florida where the sun was warm and the beaches endless. He'd hoped that by showing her how welcome she was in Silver Lake, she'd want to stay.

There was still time, he reminded himself.

"You okay?" she asked, stepping even closer.

"Ah, yeah." Daydreaming could get a soldier killed.

"How about I try to punch you and you use your tactics on me?" she asked with a sparkle to her eye that said trouble was just around the corner.

He liked that idea better because he didn't want to inadvertently hurt her. "Go for it."

Lexi planted one foot behind the other and then hauled off and hit him. Even if he hadn't moved to the side, the blow wouldn't have done much damage despite the power behind the hit. Punching techniques would have to be for another day.

With his twisting move, her fist glanced off his chest instead of hitting him dead on. Before she had a chance to draw back her arm, he stepped in close and yanked on her elbow, drawing her near. With her momentum moving forward, he stepped to the side and let her tumble to the mat.

"Hey, that's not fair," she said from on her knees. She jumped up, the small smile telling him she was merely pissed with herself that he caught her off guard.

"Fights are never fair," he threw back.

Her brows rose. "Okay, I see how it's going to be. Let's have a go again, but this time, you try to hit me."

"Sure," he said though he wouldn't use all of his power. She faced him and held up her hands in a self-defense mode. "Bend your knees. You want to keep your center of gravity low for better balance."

"Like this?" She widened her stance and thrust back her butt.

"Perfect. In order to have some power in your punch, your right foot needs to be back even farther."

"Got it. Now try me."

While Sam did a less than full speed punch, not only did Lexi twist to the side, she leaned in and then grabbed his arm to throw him off balance. At the same time, she raised her other hand to claw his face. Sam spun once more to avoid having his eyes gouged out, and then hooked his leg around hers. Down she went again. This time she landed on her butt.

With narrowed eyes, she raised up on her elbows. "You fight dirty."

She was so cute, spread out on the mat like that. "Thank you." Sam dropped to his knees and straddled her.

"I like this move though," she said as she dragged her gaze from his face right down to his crotch.

Sam had to use all of his control to rein in those blue sparks. Shit. It wasn't supposed to be sexual. "This is in case someone tries to sexually assault you."

"Oh."

"What would you do?" he asked, wanting her to think about her vulnerable position.

"Fight like hell."

"Show me." She drew her knees toward her chest and tried to kick him, but he held down her arms. "Okay, stop struggling. Your instincts are good, but your first mistake was not pressing your hands on my shoulders to keep me from getting closer."

Sam could feel his blue sparks rise to the surface once more, and he had to look at the red mat beside her to calm down. As soon as he let go of her arms, Lexi grabbed his shoulders. "Like this?"

"Yes. Now, twist to the side in order to place one foot on my hip. It's called shrimping out. In a real situation, slam your heel hard against the man. Try it."

Lexi was a fast learner. Not only did she twist to one side and plant her foot in the right spot, she repeated the maneuver on the other side. "Now what?"

"Look how you've stopped me. Even if I try to lean forward, your arms and feet are preventing me from getting too close." He demonstrated, and she managed to keep him at a safe distance. "Note that with not much effort I can elbow your arms out of the way." He twisted and disengaged her stiff arm. He then sat back. "To keep me from doing that, draw in your legs then kick my body and my head. Your goal is to keep me from wanting to get close."

"Okay, but I'll go slow. I don't want to hurt you."

Sam couldn't help but smile at her protective nature. "Thank you." With great agility, Lexi managed to drive her foot into his chin, stopping right before taking his head off. He rolled off her. "Excellent."

"I didn't know that fighting could be so much fun," she said.

"It's only fun when your opponent isn't trying to kill you, but I'll admit you're good."

"I'm strong too."

He didn't want her to become too cocky. "For a woman, you are, but an extra fifty or sixty pounds weight advantage can swing the balance against you."

Still on the mat, she turned onto her side to face him. Her eyes had turned a lighter shade and random sparks were flying off her. The words *danger, danger* flashed before his eyes. As much as he wanted a repeat of that kiss on the mountain, he'd never be able to stop this time if she kissed him full on.

She reached out and clasped his shoulder. "You're a good teacher."

"You're a better student."

Just as Sam was about to push up and get the hell out of the danger zone, Lexi cupped his cheek and kissed him once more. Even with her eyes closed to block out those alluring golden orbs, his insides exploded with need. This wasn't good, though his cock sure as hell liked what was happening.

As much as he wanted to press her to his chest and make love with her, Sam wouldn't. He respected her too much. When Lexi tried to tease open his lips, Sam's control nearly broke. He leaned back, and her eyes flew open.

"Why did you stop?" she asked. This time, her anger had risen to the surface.

Aw, shit. "Lexi, you've been through a lot."

"That's why a little kissing and touching could go a long way to helping me heal."

He blew out a breath. "It's not that simple. You're vulnerable, and I don't want you to get hurt."

She sat up and glanced to the side. "I get it. You're not into me."

He wanted to say that wasn't true. In fact, he liked her too much, but to say he felt a mating pull might cause her to make choices that would not be in her best interest. From the way she was avoiding eye contact, he'd hurt her feelings, but apologizing would result in them ending up in bed. While his body was begging him for some release, the soldier in him said it would be better to take it slow.

Sam stood and held out a hand. "Come on. We have more work

to do."

Thankfully, she let him help her up. "No rest for the weary?"

From the sparkle in her eyes, she was only partially kidding. "Absolutely not, soldier!"

AS SOON AS the mystery woman left the bar, Kapok and his men began drinking hard. Devon was a bit surprised that Kapok didn't go after his lady friend, especially after she threw out the challenge about him not being able to handle her. From the way she'd danced with him so seductively, they had a close relationship. Perhaps Kapok wanted to save face in front of his men by showing that no woman really mattered.

Not wanting to appear as if Devon was following Kapok, he paid for his drinks and food and left. While waiting in the car would suck, if something were about to go down, he couldn't afford to let Justin get the slip on him.

A boring hour later, the whole crew emerged. All but Kapok glanced around. Instead, the kingpin headed straight for his Hummer. The rest surveyed the lot. Devon immediately turned off his engine so as not to attract attention. Had it not been so freaking cold and windy in Vermont, he wouldn't have had to keep the engine running in the first place.

Kapok sat in his car a few minutes before leaving, possibly debating whether to head home or stop off for a booty call with his woman. His men, however, waited in the lot another twenty minutes after he left.

Devon wouldn't have pegged Kapok as the paranoid type. What was the man up to? Was he into drug smuggling, guns, or human trafficking? Perhaps he was running a gambling scam and feared he'd be caught. It didn't matter which vices had their hold on him, he was a man with power, and he liked to exploit that fact.

Jackson had already provided Devon with Kapok's address, so he could afford to keep his distance and sit tight until the posse left.

Once they'd cleared out, Devon drove straight to Kapok's house where his Hummer sat in front of an unlit home. Guess the man had called it a night.

Because Devon already had a long, tiring day, he went to a cheap hotel on the edge of town. His goal was to grab a few hours sleep and then return tomorrow morning for a fun-filled day of sitting in his cold car watching Kapok. As much as he enjoyed his job, surveillance was the worst part.

After a so-so sleep, he drove back to Kapok's house the next morning to ensure he was still in town. He was. In fact, his car hadn't moved. Good. Devon wasn't up for any kind of chase until he'd had something to eat. Quite hungry, Devon left and found a local diner where he could refuel before another long day of keeping watch over Lexi's stalker.

As he was waiting for the waitress to notice him, the door opened, and the hairs on his body stood at attention. Devon whipped around, not believing that the same beautiful vision from the bar last night was here. Whoa. She might not be as put together as she had been last night, but she would still turn any man's head.

His vision-woman looked rather distraught, causing his protective mechanism to shoot into high gear. She must have sensed him watching, because when her gaze reached him, she broke into a smile and rushed over. His pulse raced with need the closer she came.

"Hi," she said, twisting her hands together. "Weren't you at the Bull's Head Bar last night?" Without asking permission, she slid in opposite him, and his vocal cords seemed to have closed up.

"Uh-uh."

She set a ratty looking purse on the table. "Look. I know you don't know me, but I'm in trouble, and you seem like a nice guy who might be able to help."

Devon sat up straighter. What had he done to indicate he was that kind of person? No one could have made him. He'd been careful. "What kind of trouble?"

"I am such an idiot." She stuck out her hand. "Sorry, I'm

Vinea."

He shook her hand. "Devon."

"That's a nice name." She glanced to the side, acting shy— nothing like the confident woman from last night.

"Thanks. Tell me what happened."

She blew out a breath. "It's a bit embarrassing, but I've been conned."

The waitress came over, handed them menus, and then asked if they'd like coffee. Vinea's eyes lit up. "Yes please."

Devon nodded that he needed a refill. She poured the hot brew and then disappeared, presumably to let them decide what they wanted. "You were saying?" he asked.

"The man I was with last night, Justin Kapok, promised me a ride out of town. Only when I got to his house this morning, he'd taken off with all my stuff." Her bottom lip trembled.

Kapok must have left right after Devon checked on him. As much as Devon wanted to ask questions about Kapok, he couldn't afford to blow his cover. For all he knew, this beautiful woman worked for him and had made up a story to get him to say why he was checking on the man. "That really sucks. You don't have his number so you can call him?"

"I do, but he has my phone."

That wasn't looking good for her. "What are you planning to do?"

"I have to find a way to go after him."

"Is what he took worth it?" He couldn't blurt out and warn her that Kapok was a dangerous man.

She looked off to the side and swiped a finger under her eye. "Other than one suitcase I have with me, he has everything I own. I was moving to Tennessee to be with my sister, and he promised to take me."

If she was that poor, what was she doing in such a fancy outfit last night? Something didn't add up. "How much stuff did you have?" All of his possessions would overflow a big truck let alone a

Hummer.

"Four suitcases. I'd lost my job in New Hampshire and had to sell my jewelry and everything of value just to pay for a place to stay."

"What kind of job did you have?" Devon didn't want to speculate.

"I was working in an Indian Casino. Justin would come in and sit at my table. I thought he was cute. After a while, I wanted him to like me, so I gave him a better card than his opponent from time to time."

"And the managers found out and canned you." It was a statement rather than a question.

She placed her hands on her lap. "Yes. Justin felt so bad that he offered to help me out. He said he'd drive me to Tennessee since he was headed there anyway."

"You don't have a car?"

"Not really. I mean I have a car, but it's an old one I borrowed from a friend. I need to give it back."

This conversation was becoming more bizarre. "What part of Tennessee?"

"My sister lives halfway between Chattanooga and Knoxville."

His mind spun. "Is that where this Justin guy was headed?"

"He's going to some place called Silver Lake, which he said wasn't far from where my sister lives."

What? How could Kapok possibly know that was where Lexi was? Had one of his men followed her? "You said he already left?"

"Yes."

Devon wasn't sure what she thought he could do, but he did want to help in case she was telling the truth. He fished out his wallet and dropped two hundred dollars on the table. This poor woman had really fallen on hard times. "Here, go buy a bus ticket with this."

A smile the size of a large football field broke out on her face. "Are you kidding me?"

"Just get to your sister's safely."

"You bet I will. I'll never be able to thank you."

Feeling overly proud of himself, he pulled out one of his business cards. "If you need help, contact me."

"McKinnon and Associates. You're a security expert?" He nodded. "Do I know how to pick 'em or what?"

# Chapter Eight

WHEN SAM CAME into work the next morning, Connor was in the process of showing Lexi how to access the group calendar. "Each man logs in daily here, and then he estimates how much more time he might need to complete the case. You can tell which of the men are available to take on the next job," Connor explained.

Sam stepped close to her on the other side and instantly realized his mistake of being so near. Lexi's lemony scent made his hands tingle, forcing him to hide them behind his back. Hopefully, she didn't spot his blue sparks.

Exhausted from not having slept last night, his control had slipped. He just couldn't get those kisses they'd shared out of his head, from when they were at the top of the mountain to the one they'd shared after they had sparred. Sam pushed those erotic thoughts back and focused. "If you click on this tab at the bottom, you can see the individual schedules. The problem is that we often help each other out, and then don't fill out the form," Sam said.

"We're working on that," Connor said, shooting him a fake evil stare. Connor was just as bad at updating the schedule as the rest of them.

She smiled. "I understand. Basically, if some customer wants to hire one of the men to say check on someone, I would use this calendar to see who's most likely to be finishing a job or who has nothing on his plate."

"Exactly." Connor's cell rang, and he pulled the phone from his pocket. "Excuse me. It's Devon." He tapped the screen. "What did you learn? You sure? What do you know about her?" Connor turned his back, preventing Sam from making out the conversation. From the way Lexi's eyes had widened, she could hear every word.

Connor disconnected and faced him. "The news isn't good."

"Justin's coming after me, isn't he?" Lexi asked, her shoulders suddenly stiff.

"Yes. Devon, my brother, found him. He learned today that he and his crew are driving down here now. He suspects Kapok will arrive in two days if not sooner."

Lexi closed her eyes for a moment, and Sam wanted nothing more than to hold her—but he wouldn't. She turned toward Sam. "What am I supposed to do now? Should I leave?"

Her voice nearly cracked. "Absolutely not. More than ever, you need to stay here. We'll find Kapok and take care of him."

"How did he know I was here? I was so careful."

"I wish I had the answer to that," Sam said.

"Remember," Connor interjected. "We can't do anything until he does something illegal."

Sam spun on his heels. "What are you suggesting? Wait until he grabs her first?"

"No, not at all. We do what we always do. We watch him. If he tries anything, we pounce. I'll have Jackson get his drone ready. I'll also ask Rye to spread the word for the Clan to be on the lookout for this man. He and his five men shouldn't be hard to spot."

Lexi reached up and clasped Connor's hand. "Thank you."

"We won't let him harm you."

She sagged back against her chair. When Connor went back to his office, Sam went over the protocol of answering the door. "If someone rings the bell, check the monitor to see who it is. If you recognize that person, press this button to let them in. If not, ask them what they want by pressing this button here. If it's a client they will have an appointment scheduled that you can verify in the calendar. Ask them to have a seat in the lobby, and then either call one of us, or come get us, though we prefer that you not leave your station."

"Do you think I should have a gun?" she said with such a serious expression, she looked closer to eighteen than twenty-five.

Sam smiled. "Not yet."

"Like I said yesterday, I would like to learn." Her brows pinched, and her chest expanded. He called it her defiant look. Or maybe it should be called her don't-mess-with-me look.

"Training takes time. Once you have your permit, we'll talk, but guns aren't all they're cracked up to be. You have to be willing to use them. Should Kapok come to the door, just don't let him in. Call one of us, and we'll deal with him."

"How about if he sneaks in?" she asked, smugness lacing her tone.

"I don't know how he can, unless he keeps out of camera range and then dashes in when you open the door for someone else. If that happens, I suggest you shift and attack."

She crossed her arms over her chest. "If I can get to one of the rooms with the fingerprint scanner, I'd be safer."

"Let's hope it doesn't come to that, but I will remind Jackson to get you clearance."

Lexi reached out and squeezed his hand. "I really appreciate what you've done for me. I just want this to end as quickly as possible. I can't hide my whole life."

"It'll only be for a few more days. I imagine, Justin will arrive in town and try to find you. When he can't, he'll move on."

"Let's hope."

Sam nodded to her computer. "Are you good?"

"Yes. I can answer the phone, and I know how to forward the call to any one of you."

Because Lexi looked so defeated, he leaned over and kissed her forehead. "Enjoy your day. Just think, you could be dumpster diving."

That earned him a smile. "You won't ever let me live that down, will you?"

"Never."

Now that she was safe, Sam headed into Connor's office. His boss was at his computer. When Connor spotted Sam, he stopped what he was doing and leaned back in his chair. "Is Lexi all set?"

"Yes. What did Devon say exactly?"

"Nothing much. He met some woman who claimed Kapok left this morning to drive to Silver Lake."

"For real? How convenient to find such a valuable source. Did he have time to verify she was who she claimed, and not some mole working for Kapok?"

Connor scrubbed a hand down his face. "After she gave him the information, Devon tried to check her story, but he said he couldn't."

"But he believed her when she said Kapok was headed here?"

"Apparently. Devon said he was able to verify that she did get fired from her former job as a casino dealer."

Sam supposed it didn't matter who the source was. Bottom line, everyone needed to be ready when Kapok arrived. "I'd like to know how he figured out Lexi was here. She said she didn't use her phone or credit cards."

Connor tapped his desk. "Could he have installed a tracking device on her car?"

"When would he have had time? According to Lexi, her father told her he planned to hand her over to Kapok. A few minutes later she left town. Even Lexi didn't know she'd run out of gas in Silver Lake."

"He could have placed it on her car a few days before. We don't know when this card game occurred. Why don't you check out her vehicle? Uncle Garth said she could keep the car behind the pub until she was ready to drive it, but it might be safer here."

"Sounds good. Let me see if Jackson can help. He's better at that stuff than I am." Connor's brows rose, acting like Sam was some car expert and could find it easily. "What? A tracking device is not a bomb. That I can handle. I might even be able to figure out the source of the knocking, but I don't deal in all kinds of security devices and what they look like. Besides, Jackson has that device that can sweep for bugs."

Connor chuckled. "True. Watch what he does so you can learn. After all, this is a security firm. Go. I'll make sure someone is always in the office so Lexi remains safe."

"Thanks. When does your dad come home from his trip?" Connor's father and Jackson's dad had built this building so that when they were in town, they'd have an office here. They both said they missed working.

"Next week. We can use both of them on this case."

He agreed. The more eyes on the lookout for this man the better. Sam headed back down the hallway to find Jackson, only he wasn't there, so he called him. Jackson said he'd stayed up late doing some surveillance work but promised he'd be there shortly. "Do you think you could help me out when you get here?"

"Sure. What do you need?"

Once he filled him in, Sam returned to the reception area to speak with Lexi.

"Hey," she said with a smile. "You find out anything more?"

Sam placed a hip on the corner of her desk. "Not really. Assuming, you didn't use a credit card or call someone, the only way Justin could have found you was if he put a tracking device on your car." He wouldn't suggest that Kapok might have had her watched for a few days before she left town or that his men might have followed her. If Kapok's men had been trained by the military, she would never have spotted them.

She slapped a hand on his chest. "When would he have done that? I left minutes after finding out what my father had done."

Sam hadn't meant to upset her. "It's just a theory that I'm about to test. Jackson is on his way over here. Together, we're going to figure it out, but don't worry. Connor will be here if you need anything."

She blew out a long breath. "I guess if there is a device, we need to remove it." She pulled out a drawer and extracted her purse. "Here are the keys in case you need them."

"Thanks. If we find the device, we'll consider placing it on some vehicle with out of state plates. Once they leave town, they'll give Kapok a good run for his money."

Lexi smiled, and his pulse sped up. "What I wouldn't give to see his face when he realized he's been fooled," she said.

Sam chuckled. "Let's see if it's there first."

"Uh-oh. I just thought of something. When I was checking my engine at the rest stop, those two guys came over to supposedly help me. Remember, I said one robbed me?"

"Yes. Do you think the first guy could have slipped something in the engine?"

"That or maybe inside the car. I had my window open to air it out, despite it being cold."

"Let's hope we get lucky." Without touching or kissing her, he returned to the main area. Once Sam grabbed his jacket from his office, he left by the side door in order to grab a can of gasoline from the storage locker. As he exited the shed, Jackson pulled up in his Silverado truck and waved.

Sam placed the gas can in the bed of Jackson's truck and hopped in. "Good timing," Sam said.

"So you think Lexi's car was bugged?"

He told him about the two men who robbed her. "One could have put something in the engine when she wasn't looking or the other guy could have planted it when he reached in to steal her money. Kapok probably suspected she might run. To ensure his investment remained within reach, he installed the device."

"Any of those scenarios sound plausible. Give me a sec, and I'll run in and get my bug sweeper."

"Thanks."

Once Jackson returned, Sam filled him in on Devon's call. "I'm thinking the drone might be able to help," Sam said.

"I'll be happy to fire it up. I'll need a make and model of the vehicle he's driving."

"Your Clan is on the case, but he owns a Hummer. While this Vinea woman implied Kapok had driven his vehicle, I wouldn't put it past him to switch cars or take someone else's."

"That would cramp our ability to find him."

When they arrived behind the pub, Sam was relieved her car was where she'd left it. "I'll give it some gas while you check for the tracking devices."

"Thanks for giving me the dirty job, though this will get it done faster."

"You'll have to show me how to use it some time," Sam said.

"Will do."

Once Sam emptied the can, he slid into the driver's seat and fired up the engine. It sputtered for a second before roaring to life. Before he hopped out, he ran his hand under the dash trying to find something that didn't belong. Failing, he got out. "Any luck?" he asked Jackson.

"Nope." His co-worker was on his back in the snow checking under the chasse. He slid out a moment later. "I'll check under the hood too."

Sam popped the hood. "Let me try."

Jackson gave him a quick tutorial on the scanner. Sam ran the machine around waiting for the light to turn red, indicating there was a device. "I got nothing."

"That means someone probably followed her," Jackson said.

Sam didn't like it. "It looks like it. Thanks for your help. I'll drive the car back and park it inside the garage. We don't need Kapok spotting it." They had a four-bay garage. Two spots were only used when the two elders were in town. The other two spaces were for anyone who needed to keep his car out of sight.

Jackson nodded. "I'll stop in and let Garth know we have the car."

"Appreciate it." Once Sam returned to the office, he told Lexi they didn't find anything.

"Then how did he find me?"

Sam explained his theory about possibly being followed.

"I checked my rear view constantly. Sure, there were cars behind me, but when I got off at an intersection, it wasn't like they followed me to the rest stop." She sucked in a breath. "Damn. It was them. Those guys who robbed me must have been working with Justin. They took my money to force me to resort to using my credit cards in case they lost track of me."

"It seems the most likely case."

"Then I should leave—like in the middle of the night."

"No!" Sam hadn't meant his voice to rise. "Who's to say his men aren't out there right now waiting for you to make your move?"

"Are you trying to scare me even more?"

Sam didn't seem to be able to do anything right. "How can you say that? I just want to keep you safe."

Lexi slumped against her chair. "I know you are. It's just that I feel like I'm in prison." She held up her palm. "Albeit a wonderfully comfortable one with gracious hosts."

"It sucks, I know. While you try to lose yourself in the joys of your job, our team will figure something out."

She blew out a breath and tossed the pen in her hand on the desk. "You're right. So when did you say you're going to teach me to shoot a gun?"

Sam laughed, enjoying her spirit. "Let's master your learning to deal with customers first."

She saluted and returned her gaze to the computer.

As Sam headed off, he wondered if he was doing right by her. If he weren't convinced she was his mate, he'd find a way to sneak her out of town. After they vanquished Justin Kapok, Sam would have to figure out if Lexi felt the same way about him that he felt about her.

LEXI WANTED TO hit something—or rather someone—namely Justin. If he knew where she was, why wasn't he making his move? He should have arrived three days ago, yet no one had seen him. This waiting for the other shoe to drop was killing her. Sam told her that Rye McKinnon's Clan said no one had even reported anyone asking for her.

Had the whole thing been an elaborate hoax by Justin to pay her back for running away? Maybe he realized that an unwilling woman wouldn't serve his purpose. If his goal was to breed, he'd need some cooperation on her part, which she certainly wouldn't get. Then again, he might resort to force. At that thought she shivered.

Thinking about mating and having children, her thoughts instantly jumped to Sam. Had the circumstances been different, Sam would be the man for her. He'd make a loving and protective father to her kids. That much she was sure.

The office phone rang, giving her a chance to take her mind off her problems—and the sexy Sam Pompley. "McKinnon and Associates."

"I'm in need of an investigator."

"We can certainly help." She went through a series of questions that Connor had written down for her in order to help her decide who might be best suited for a potential client. "Just a moment and I'll see who's free." She looked over the calendar and the only person who wasn't on a job was Sam. "I'll patch you through."

"Thanks."

Once she'd made the transfer, she glanced over at the pile of paperwork waiting to be filed. She walked over to the table they'd set up for her, along with the file cabinet. As she looked over the papers, an idea struck her. What if she made a spreadsheet of every client, along with every person they'd ever interviewed? She'd assign key words so that cross-referencing them would be easier. Perfect. Excited that she'd be more than a secretary with little to do, she set about her task.

Once she figured out how to organize the names, she questioned if she should give up on the idea of leaving Silver Lake. Not only was she totally safe locked away in here, this was a good job. While it could be boring if she let it, if she used her math skills, she could become a valuable asset to the team members. Another perk was that she would be paid weekly. And then there were all these hot men running around, like Sam.

*Sam.*

Her wolf was growing more desperate each day, but if she let herself indulge in what he had to offer, when it came time to leave, it would make it worse for both of them. If she thought danger wouldn't touch him too, she'd consider making Silver Lake her home.

Before she could think further on the topic, the front door buzzer sounded, and she nearly jumped out of her skin. Her train of thought derailed as her hand shook. She pressed the button to see who was there. A man, neatly groomed, wearing a large overcoat was there. "May I help you?"

"The name's Frisch. I have an appointment with Kip Landon."

"Just a moment please," said Lexi as she checked her screen and spotted the appointment then buzzed him in.

"Mr. Frisch, have a seat, and I'll notify Mr. Landon that you're here." Even though this wasn't Justin, her heart was still pounding in her chest.

Two minutes later, Kip came out to greet the man and then ushered him to his office. By the time five o'clock rolled around, her official duties were over. Just as she was about to head on down to her little cave, Connor strolled in and handed her an envelope.

"What's this?" she asked.

"Your first week's pay."

Lexi's hands shook. It would be impolite to count the money in front of him, but she was curious how much they paid. Instead of satisfying her curiosity, she stuffed the money in her purse. "Thank you."

No sooner had Connor returned to the inner sanctum than

Jackson breezed in, bringing with him the fresh scent of cold winter air. "Lexi."

"Jackson."

"Going stir crazy yet?" he asked with a smile.

"I'm keeping busy, but I can't help but wonder when Justin will make his move." Sam wasn't as open about discussing what was happening as he was.

"Be patient. Kapok won't wait too long. If he's here, he's not gambling. Not gambling means lost wages."

She hadn't thought of that. "True. He's probably waiting for me to go outside. Perhaps I should walk down one of the main streets with you guys standing by ready to pounce."

"That would be dangerous. You know Sam; he'd have a fit."

"I know. He acts like he owns me." Not that there wasn't an upside to that, but right now, it was hard to breathe easily with him hovering all the time.

Jackson winced. "He cares about you, that's all."

"I know, but I want some freedom."

"You two will work it out. If anyone asks, I'm on my way up to the roof to send out my drone in the hopes of spotting Kapok or his men."

"Do you know what kind of car he's driving?"

"He left Vermont in a Hummer. Whether he still has it is anyone's guess."

A few minutes after Jackson disappeared down the hallway, Sam came in from the back. Why she'd thought things were slow, she didn't know. "You want to grab some dinner?" he asked.

Had he been listening to her conversation with Jackson, or had Jackson found Sam and told him to take her out? "You mean you're actually letting me out of my cage?"

Pain skated across his face. He lifted her up by the shoulders. "What do you want me to do? Encourage you to go out and shop by yourself?"

If she had money to spare, she'd like nothing better. "What do you think about letting me go into town in order to draw out Justin? You could be nearby making sure he doesn't harm me."

He shook his head. "We'd need a lot of men for that, and even then something might happen. If he remains hidden for another few days, we might consider it." Sam clutched her to his chest, and many of her worries melted away. He leaned back. "I know being cooped up here isn't fun. I have a spare bedroom. Do you want to spend the night there? I have windows in my house."

Not only did her pulse race, heat swept over her body at what might happen. "I'd love nothing more than a change of scenery." If he thought for one minute that being offered different sleeping arrangements would stop her from seducing him, he was crazy.

# Chapter Nine

"LET ME PACK a few things," Lexi said to Sam. For the first time in days, she was excited about life. No, she had to take that back. When she and Sam had gone snowmobiling, she'd really felt alive!

After rushing down the hallway, she ducked into the office that led to her secret staircase, and her heart sputtered at seeing someone hunched over a computer. It took a second for her to realize it was probably Devon. "Oh, sorry. I forgot this was your office when you're in town." He was lucky to get a flight back to town so fast.

His smile reminded her of Connor's. "No problem. You must be Lexi. I'm Devon." He held out her hand and she shook it.

"Nice to meet you."

"I trust you need to get to your lair?"

She appreciated his sense of humor. "Yes. Sam and I are headed out to dinner and then we're going over to his place. He thinks I could use a change of scenery."

His brows rose. "A night of freedom. Nice." He scooted out of the way. "I guess my dad wasn't thinking when he put the secret hideaway at the back of an office."

"Maybe he was. Who would think to check in here?"

He lifted a finger then pointed it at her. "Good point."

Not wanting to keep Sam waiting, she stepped behind Devon then moved the four books to the side in order to press the button. This extra security made her feel so safe. Once the doors swung open,

Lexi rushed to her room, grabbed her only suitcase and tossed in a few items. With her coat tossed over her arm, she returned.

"Later," she said as she headed to the door. The fact Devon was still around implied everyone believed Justin's threat was real. She swung around to face him. "Thanks again for flying up to Vermont."

He waved a hand. "I enjoyed it. I was able to help another lady in need, which made me feel good."

She hadn't realized men like these even existed—so protective and good hearted.

Nodding, she headed out to meet Sam who was waiting by the front door for her. "Ready?" he asked.

"You bet."

She slipped on her coat while he grabbed her suitcase and then motioned her out. Once outside, the cold wind bit into her skin, but it reminded her that she was alive. "So where are we going for dinner?"

"Some place special. It's called the Lake Steakhouse."

Lexi grinned and wrapped an arm around his. "Sounds wonderful."

Ten minutes later they were parked in front of the restaurant, but Sam made her wait in the truck until he'd checked out the area. Did he think Justin would be pacing up and down the street waiting for her? When they did meet, Justin would probably just talk to her about returning to Vermont with him. Of course, she'd say no. Only after that attempted failure did she envisioned him turning violent.

Sam held open her truck door. "We're good."

"He's not going to attack on a busy street, you know."

"Let's hope," Sam said and then escorted her inside.

The restaurant was more upscale than she'd expected. The open view of the kitchen and the nice bar area made it classy but cozy. Their hostess escorted them to a table. "This place looks expensive," Lexi whispered.

He smiled. "That's why it's my treat."

She let out a small laugh. "Good, because I can't afford it."

He placed a hand on her back, and her body immediately reacted. *Please don't let any blue sparks erupt.* Thinking about Justin for a moment calmed her down. That was close.

Once seated, her pulse began to slow. The white table cloth and lit candle helped calm her. Lexi didn't know all that much about Sam and wanted to find out more. "So what made you go into the service?"

He shook out his white napkin and placed it on his lap. It was almost as if he needed time to compose his thoughts. "My dad served, but after one four-year stint, he met my mom. Because she wanted to start a family, he decided not to reenlist, but he liked to tell stories about his time in the service. Those really resonated with me."

"That's kind of sweet."

His brows rose. "Maybe. My mom was into anything that had to do with the paranormal and the supernatural. Even though both of my parents are Wendayan and have powers, Dad was more straight-laced. Once my mom got a hold of him though, he changed."

"Can your dad control a person's mind?"

"No, but his father could. My dad could change the shape of things to suit his need. Like if a box was slightly too small, he could make it bigger."

"I bet that comes in handy."

"It does, though he rarely uses his magic, fearing someone might see him."

"What do they do now?"

"When I was about ten, both of my parents decided to devote their lives to healing the soul and exploring the spiritual elements in life. It might have been a bit of rebellion on my part that made me want to serve, because I didn't want to follow in their psychic ways, despite having a bent in that direction. I wanted something more grounded—if that's the right word."

Her pulse sped up. "I totally understand. I think that's why I ended up studying math. There isn't any ambiguity in science like there is in witchcraft. Being a shape shifter is bad enough, but then add in my other talents, and all I yearned for was some normalcy. Mind you, my Wendayan talents are nothing like yours. Hell, it's almost like I don't have any." She mouthed a few of the words to make sure no one heard.

"That's not true. You're strong and agile."

"Compared to you, I'm not. In a fight, I'm not sure it will be much of an advantage."

"We need to continue working on that. Have you done any weight training? You might improve faster than most."

She'd never had the time or the funds to join a gym, but if Sam would help train her, she was game. "No, but I'd like that!"

Their server stopped by and Sam ordered a bottle of wine for them. This seemed more than just a feed-the-poor-girl dinner. It felt like a date—a real one. "You planning on seducing me later? Is that the reason for the wine?" she joked.

When his face turned red, Lexi wished she could take back the words. "Is that what you want?" he asked.

Touché. Now it was her face heating up, but she was glad the topic had been broached. "I wouldn't turn you down if that's what you mean."

Sam let out a laugh. "You are something else, do you know that?"

Lexi didn't know whether to be insulted or flattered. It didn't matter; she'd find the right time to explore him in the very intimate way she desired. Keeping a strong seal on her heart and her wolf in check would be the real challenge.

The waiter returned with their wine and then took their order. Lexi decided on something simple—prime rib and potatoes while Sam chose the rib eye steak with mushrooms on top.

"Have you called your brother yet?" Sam asked as he sampled his wine.

"I finally did last night. I didn't want him to worry."

"Does he know about Justin?"

She nodded. "Yes. I told him when I asked him for my escape money. Ronan asked where I was, but I said it would worry me less if he didn't know. I certainly don't need him down here looking for revenge against someone as powerful as Justin. My brother would want to play Mr. Protector, and I already have plenty of them here."

"That you do."

"I explained that I was in good hands, and he agreed to stay put, though he wasn't happy about it. I kept all names out of it."

"I trust you didn't contact your father?"

She barked out a laugh. "That would be a no."

The waiter returned. "Mr. Pompley?"

"Yes."

"You have a phone call at the hostess stand."

Sam glanced at her. "Other than Connor, I didn't believe anyone knew we were here." He patted his pants and extracted his phone.

"I told Devon we were going out, but not where." Lexi nodded to his cell. "Did he leave a message?"

"No. Nothing. My phone has plenty of charge too. I can't imagine who it would be. It must be Connor."

As soon as Sam left, a wave of melancholy descended. She liked being with him. Not only did he provide a sense of security, his mere presence helped calm her.

*That's because he's our mate, silly,* her wolf called out.

*That may be, but mating with him would be too dangerous—for him.*

Having sex, however, was in the cards. Mating right now? Probably not.

Just as she turned around to check on him, a loud blast sent her world spinning. People screamed and then smoke rolled down the corridor to where she was seated. Oh, my goddess. Sam!

SAM COULDN'T EXPLAIN why he stopped before reaching the hostess station. Perhaps it was because the hostess wasn't there, or else his sixth sense kicked into high gear. It was the same weird feeling he'd had when he and his men were supposed to enter an Afghani building that claimed to house a terrorist cell. At the last minute, he called off the mission and sent in a robot instead. They'd attached a tall antenna to the machine to simulate a human. Sure enough, it hit an electronic trigger and the building exploded.

He'd just turned around to return to Lexi, a bomb exploded behind him. His heart nearly jumped out of his chest as a blast sent shockwaves through the air, forcing him to shield his face from any flying debris.

A few seconds later, he regained his bearings, and his first instinct was to make sure Lexi was okay. Justin might have created this diversion in order to take her. His heart lurched. Smoke entombed him, but the lack of heat implied there wasn't a fire.

Sam charged against the stream of the screaming crowd who were trying to exit the front where the blast had occurred, while a few were running toward the back. If the smoke hadn't been so dense, he'd have a better idea what had occurred.

"Lexi?" he shouted. His heart pounded as he tried to find their table. "Lexi!"

Not only was his vision impaired, chairs had toppled, blocking his way. Angry and scared voices obliterated his ability to hear if she answered. A lot of pushing and shoving made it difficult to even find the tables and booths.

Someone grabbed his arm, and he spun around. "Sam, it's me!"

Thank God, it was Lexi. "Are you okay?"

She coughed. "Yes, you?" She handed him his jacket, but he didn't take the time to put it on.

Thank goodness for her shifter vision or she might not have found him. "I'm fine. Let's get out of here."

The lights flickered and then extinguished. More screams and panicked shouts rent the air. Fuck. Now they were blind. The crowd jostled and bumped into them, and the smoke stung his eyes. Lexi managed to stay on her feet so far, but to prevent her from falling he wrapped an arm tightly around her waist. "Hold on."

"This way," Lexi said.

Given her excellent eyesight, he let her lead. They'd moved less than ten feet when something hard slammed into his side. Anger rushed to the surface as he stumbled, but Lexi tightened her hold to prevent him from falling.

Embarrassed at nearly being knocked over, he charged forward. His lungs burned and his vision was nil. Images of Afghanistan surfaced again, but he tamped them down.

Someone grabbed his left arm and tugged. What the hell? Did they mistake him for someone else? "Let go," Sam shouted as he jerked out of that person's grasp.

Stepping over shards of wood, he and Lexi finally reached the front door, and then burst into the street. Fresh air met them. As much as he wanted to stop and ask her questions about whether she saw anything, they needed to get the hell out of there. Even in war, he hadn't seen such panic.

Unlocking the passenger side door to his truck took some doing, as the smoke had followed them outside. Add in the fact that lights in front of the restaurant were out, it made seeing difficult. Now would be a great time to have enhanced shifter sight.

Sirens sounded. Not wanting to be blocked in, he helped Lexi into the passenger's side then jumped into his seat. Seconds later, they were clear of the crowd and headed north to their office.

"What happened in there?" Lexi asked, clearly shaken.

"I was on my way to the hostess station when something inside me said not to take the call. I'm not even sure there was one."

"It sounded like something blew up." She nodded to his arm. Blood stained his sleeve. "You're cut. Are you sure you're okay?"

Her concern warmed him. "Yes. I didn't even feel it. Too much adrenaline I guess."

"Sam, do you think this had something to do with me?"

"It's possible though I was the one who was called to the front."

"What better way to get to me than to put you out of commission?"

His gut soured. "You might be right. If I went down, and if you managed to escape, Connor or Jackson could take care of you."

"That's a lot of ifs."

True. His sixth sense had saved her—this time. His mind raced to what might happen next. "I think you should stay at the office tonight."

She let out a huff. "I understand it's necessary, but I want you there with me."

"Absolutely. I'm not leaving you." His protective side was in full force. He wasn't going to leave her under any circumstance. Keeping his distance however was a given.

Right now, the urge to hold her and kiss her was strong, but with his emotions high, he had to be careful. "I'll need to stop at my place and pick up a few things."

"Sure. Can we then stop at a drive thru afterward? I'm really hungry."

They never did receive their meal. "How about I cook something at home? I'm sure you want to enjoy what little freedom I'm affording you for as long as possible."

She grinned and his heart sang. "Thank you."

While he didn't live far, Sam kept his gaze on the rear view mirror. Thankfully, no one seemed to be following him. Before he reached home, the phone rang, and he depressed a lever on the wheel. "Sam, here."

"It's Connor. What the hell happened? The news crews are all over the explosion. Are you and Lexi okay?"

"Yes." Sam brought his boss up to speed.

"It sounds like someone followed you two and then planted the device by the hostess station."

"It was probably Kapok, trying to get to Lexi." Sam turned to her. "Did you catch the name of our waiter? He told us about the phone call. He might remember who told him about the call."

"I think his name was Jacob or maybe Jack. I could be wrong. I might just have Justin's name on my brain."

"I'll check it out with the owner," Connor said. "Are you going back to the office?"

"We will after I pick up a few things at the house and fix something to eat. It's safer at the office."

"Agreed. Just be careful," his boss said.

"You can count on it."

Sam disconnected. He checked his surroundings once more before turning down his street. Using the garage remote, he opened the door. Only when it was closed, did he relax.

Lexi started to get out, but Sam wanted to be extra cautious. "Let me check the house first."

"Really? You think Justin would sneak into your house? How would he even know who you are?"

"I don't want anything to happen to you. Stay here, please?"

"Fine." Lexi sank back against the seat. "If a shifter is inside, I can sense him immediately, you know."

As much as he didn't want to expose her to danger, she was right. "Okay, but stay by my side."

She tossed him a small smile. "I will."

Together they entered his darkened house. "Anything?" he asked.

"No shifter."

Sam flicked on the light that illuminated the living room. "Stay here while I look upstairs."

Lexi grabbed his arm. "I can sense a shifter that far away. He's not here."

"I know, but I want us to be safe." For the first time since the blast, the tension released from his body.

She slipped off her jacket and placed it on the back of the living room sofa while he ran up the steps. Seeing nothing disturbed, he returned.

Lexi moved closer. "You look cold," she said.

As much as he'd enjoy a warm hug, he didn't trust himself. He tossed his jacket next to hers. "I'm okay. I guess I should have put that on."

Lexi grabbed his arm and leaned in close, disrupting his thoughts again. "You've been through a lot. How about I make you some hot tea?"

So now she was the caretaker? "That would be great, but I only have coffee."

She smiled. "Works for me."

Since she'd never been to his place, she might not be able to find what she needed. Sam followed her past the dining room table and into the kitchen. With the large pass-through window, one could still see the living room.

"The cups are in the cabinet above the sink," he said. "I'll get the coffee."

Because the kitchen was long and narrow, they almost bumped into each other twice, yet somehow it wasn't awkward. There was an ease between them he'd not remembered having with anyone else.

Once she set the cups on the counter, Lexi hopped up next to them. "When we were headed toward the door, someone seemed to yank on your arm and you almost fell. What was that about?"

"I wish I knew. Maybe that person thought I was someone else. I couldn't see who it was, partly because I was squinting to keep the smoke out of my eyes." The coffee finished perking, and he poured two cups. "Black, right?"

"Yes."

Once he fixed their drinks, he motioned they return to the living room where the seating was more comfortable. "The phone call implies they were either targeting me, or just trying to get me out of the way in order to get to you."

"It would have been easier to say there was a call for me and then pressed a gun to my back and escort me outside."

Sam's gut churned. He set his cup on the coffee table and sat on the sofa. "That's a horrible thought. If the waiter had told you that your brother was calling, would you have answered the phone?"

"No. I didn't tell him I was in Silver Lake. Even if I had, Ronan understands why it's dangerous to contact me. There'd be no reason to call."

"Are you sure? If something happened to your dad, Ronan might have tracked your whereabouts to tell you."

Lexi glanced to the side then sipped her coffee. "If dad had been murdered and I found out about it, I probably wouldn't want to discuss it with Ronan. I'm still too pissed off at my dad." She leaned her head back on the sofa. "I'm such a horrible person. I really tried to get Bill to change his ways, but he was stubborn."

"You aren't horrible. The man tried to sell you because he gambled too much. He had an addiction."

"I know, but I wish I could have loved him the way I used to."

"He changed."

"Very true."

They didn't need to be thinking about what could have been. "Bottom line, I believe the bomb was designed to take you," Sam said. The coffee had cooled enough for him to drink half the cup in one long draw.

"So now what should we do?" she asked. Sam didn't like how dejected she sounded.

"Now? We wait."

# Chapter Ten

WAITING WAS NOT Lexi's strong suit, but what choice did she have? That explosion was a message, but for some reason it didn't scream Justin. While she'd only interacted with him once, he seemed to be a straightforward kind of guy who played the odds, not someone who created elaborate plans. Cheating was his game—not blowing things up. Then again, he might be desperate.

On the drive back to Sam's house from the restaurant, she had debated leaving town that night. This wasn't Sam's fight, and he shouldn't be dragged into her issues. However, if Justin had his eyes on her right now, leaving would play right into his hands.

"Do you think anyone was seriously hurt in the explosion?" she asked.

Sam seemed to be okay. The blood on his arm had caked, implying his cuts weren't too deep.

"I don't know, but Connor and the gang are going to find out." He tapped his thighs and stood. "Ready for some food?"

"Absolutely." She stood. "I'll help."

"I wasn't going to do anything fancy. I thought I'd make some bacon and eggs. That's all. How does that sound?"

"Divine. I still want to help." The incident had upset her more than she was willing to say and cooking might help take her mind off things. "How about I do the bacon?"

He must have heard the stress in her voice. "Sure."

She also wanted to move about in order to help her think how she wanted the rest of the evening to go. It wasn't because she wanted to merely blow off steam. The sexual tension had been building for days. If Lexi didn't take things into her own hands, her wolf might come out at the most inappropriate time. One thing was for sure. Getting naked had to be part of the evening festivities.

If Sam turned her down, Lexi might break. She needed his warmth and caring, but most of all, she wanted to be with him. Mate or no mate, he was the first person she'd met who really seemed to understand her.

Her stomach grumbled, and she returned her focus to the task at hand. "If I use the microwave, what do you want me to use to cook the bacon?"

Sam smiled. "The plate is already on the counter."

Oh crap. That meant she'd spaced out. Time to get to work. Separating the strips, she placed them on the dish then covered it with a paper towel. Once she slid it into the microwave and set the timer, she leaned against the counter to watch him.

"How about I find something to clean up that cut?" she asked, still needing to be useful.

"It doesn't hurt, but I will have to treat it at some point." He unbuttoned his shirt, and when he slipped it off, she couldn't help but stare. Given it was winter, Sam often wore a lot of bulky clothes. Even this shirt hid the wonders underneath it. Broad shoulders and rippled abs drew her eyes downward.

"I'll get the supplies if you can scramble the eggs," he said.

"Be happy to."

A few minutes later, Sam returned with bandages and a bottle in his hand—along with a clean shirt. He set the items on the counter then opened the iodine bottle.

"I can do it for you," she said, turning down the heat on the eggs.

"I'm good."

She shifted her weight to one leg. "It takes two hands to put a bandage on. Besides, let me take care of you for a change."

Sam grinned, and her heart swelled. "Then I'm all yours."

She wished. "How about rinsing those cuts first?"

It didn't appear as if any fragments had been embedded in the skin, but she wanted to be safe. She just hoped everyone else was as lucky.

Sam washed his cuts then ran his fingers over one rather deep one. "This is the only one that might be a problem."

She leaned over and studied its depth. "You should go to an Urgent Care and get it checked out."

"How about wrapping it first, and if it's not improved by tomorrow, I'll go in."

From the casual way he said it, he had no intention of doing any such thing. "Fine."

The microwave dinged. The bacon was ready, but taking care of his wounds had to come first.

"I see the eggs are done. Let me take them off the burner," he said. "Then you can play doctor."

Whoops. She'd forgotten about them. The bacon could sit in the microwave. Sam returned, and after drying his arm and placing a bandage on it, she wrapped his forearm in gauze. "That should do it."

He smiled and lifted his arm as if to inspect it. "Thank you, Doctor Laramie. Now, shall we eat?"

He slipped on his new T-shirt. While disappointed to see his chest covered, the material hugged his body well.

"Absolutely." As she readied the bacon, he emptied the scrambled eggs onto a platter. Together they took the food over to the table.

No sooner had they sat down than his cell rang. "I should take this. It's Connor." He swiped a finger across the screen. "What did you learn? Was anyone hurt? Did you find a name?" He tapped his fingers on the table while he listened. "Okay, thanks. We'll return to the office after we eat."

"What did he say?" Lexi's stomach cramped.

"Two people were hospitalized, but they should be fine. One injury came from the blast and the other from being trampled."

She couldn't believe what a nightmare it had become. "Did he find out who told the waiter you had a call?"

"Our waiter, Jacob, only remembers a woman—a very beautiful one—came up to him and said the hostess told her to find me and tell me I had a phone call."

"Why would he deliver a message to a customer from someone he didn't know? Or better yet, why would the hostess ask a stranger to deliver a message?"

"I wish I knew. Connor said the guy had just started working there a few days ago."

Her mind spun. "Justin has a lot of minions. Could he have been one of his men?"

His brows rose. "I hadn't thought of that. Devon saw several men with Kapok that night in the bar. Let me call him. Maybe he can head on over to the restaurant and identify who the man was."

"Good thinking."

Sam dialed his number.

Even though it was evening, these men didn't seem to rest. Their job was twenty-four-seven. "If he is Justin's man, this Jacob guy will disappear," she said before Devon answered.

He smiled. "You'd make a good investigator." He looked away. "Yeah, Dev. I want to pass something by you."

His compliment made her insides tingle. In the last few years, she hadn't received much in the way of positive reinforcement. While Ronan had always been supportive, her dad had not been—unless her actions benefitted him.

"I assume you heard about the explosion? Good. Lexi has an idea." He explained how the man who'd just been hired remembered that a woman told him about the phone call. "Can you check him out to see if he might be one of Kapok's men? Great. Let me know. Oh, and talk to the hostess. Supposedly, she spoke to the woman too." He disconnected. "He promised to call if he learned anything."

"Which means more waiting."

"Yes, but hopefully, you won't be too bored being in my company," he said.

*Never!*

# Chapter Eleven

LEXI DIDN'T WANT to think anymore about this whole terrible situation. Without saying a word, she tried to force down her meal, and while it tasted good, her mind couldn't stop wandering back to all that had happened. She hoped Justin wouldn't try to get to her through Sam. The last thing she wanted was anyone else in danger because of her.

If Justin was hanging around town, it might mean he had learned that she and Sam were working together, and had even gone snowmobiling. Justin would want to make sure the two of them didn't mate.

She pushed back her chair. "Let me help with the cleanup."

Sam stood and grasped her arm. "Are you okay? You seem jumpy. No one is going to hurt you."

"I know, but I can't stop thinking about everything that has happened." Wanting to halt those swirling thoughts, she stepped into his embrace and pressed her face against his chest. Even through the new shirt, his skin smelled of smoke. To her surprise, she kind of liked the outdoorsy smell.

*Mate*, her wolf growled.

Whether it was the stress, or just plain lust, she had to taste him. Lexi wrapped her arms around his neck and kissed him. Sam's lips were soft yet possessive. When his tongue traced the crease of her mouth, she let him in. The moment their tongues made contact, her wolf cheered. Sam Pompley was all man, and for the moment, all hers. Sparks flew, and she was pretty sure they didn't all come from her. Lexi couldn't be happier.

After several seconds, Sam pulled back and looked into her eyes. He ran his thumb across her bottom lip then slid his fingers up the edge of her jaw to tuck her hair behind her ear. "I want you so badly, Lexi, but I don't want to rush you. Are you sure you want to take this further right now?" he asked.

Joy burst inside her. "More than sure. I want to be with you in every way. I need you Sam, please."

He pulled her closer. "I need you too, baby."

Lexi tilted her lips up and connected with his again. It was what every girl dreamed of—passionate, strong, and needy.

As his hands roamed down the sides of her breasts to her waist and then around to the small of her back, his touch set her body on fire. Her scalp itched as her hair thickened, and her teeth turned sharper.

He slid his fingers downward until he was cupping her ass. Lexi pushed her crotch against his very impressive erection and ran her palms down his pecs and over his abs, loving the way his muscles moved the tighter he held her. Wrapping her arms around his neck again, she scraped her nails up the back of his head. The pressure and speed of the kiss increased, as did their moans and groans.

*Strip him naked*, her wolf demanded. *Mate with him now!*

As much as she'd like to make things permanent, there were too many reasons to wait. That didn't mean she couldn't rip off his clothes and enjoy him though. She stepped back. "I need you naked."

Sam raised an eyebrow and grinned at her. "Oh I will definitely be doing that, but sweetheart, yours are coming off first, and that is not a request."

His authoritative tone stopped her. Then again, he was used to being in charge. That was fine by her as long as the result ended in them getting naked and sweaty.

"As you wish." As slowly as she could, Lexi undid the top button of her shirt. When he edged forward, his eyebrows rose in a silent order of *I'm waiting*. She undid the rest of the buttons and then slipped her shirt over her shoulders, letting it fall to the floor. As his gaze followed the material, Lexi reached around her back and unhooked her pink lace bra, and Sam's gaze zeroed in on her chest. Slower than glaciers could move, she lowered one strap and then the next. Sam licked his lips, and she swore the area covering his cock glowed blue. After letting the bra join her shirt, she undid the zipper on her jeans and leisurely wiggled out of them. When she bent over to step out of her pants, Sam made a grab for her and scooped her up in his arms.

"I can't take it any longer." He placed her on the sofa, dragged off her jeans along with her panties, and flung them back, clearing the end of the couch. "Goddess in heaven, but you are a beautiful sight."

Sam stood and was out of his jeans and briefs in record time. He lost the shirt a second later.

Her gaze shot straight between his legs, and her eyes practically popped out of her head. "Whoa, do you have a special license to carry that? Talk about a concealed weapon." Lexi grinned at him.

Sam winked back. "Maybe you should make sure it's locked and loaded."

She loved his humor. "Bring it here and I'll check it out." Thankfully, she was on the pill. Because he was her mate, she saw no reason to ask him to put on protection.

Sam sat on the leather sofa then lifted her by the waist. As he set her down on his lap, she straddled him. Lexi stared at his cock pressed between them then dragged her gaze up his body, locking her eyes with his hooded gaze.

"I need to taste you," Sam said.

She thought he was asking for a kiss, but instead he placed his hand on her back and dipped her. He then licked and sucked on one nipple, sending her into oblivion. She closed her eyes and inhaled his woodsy scent, loving how her body thrilled to his touch. After he tugged on the tip with his teeth, he pulled away and blew a cool breath across it. Not only did her sparks fly, bolts of electricity shot down her body and ignited her core. For a moment, she thought she might shift, but then her wolf stood down.

Lexi slid forward and then wiggled her butt on his cock. The urge to take him right then overwhelmed her. Because much of the anticipation for making love was the foreplay, she had planned to delay for as long as possible, but Lexi wasn't sure she could last much longer. If she could, the final coupling would be a monumental event.

As he continued to suck on her tits, twisting and then pulling each tip taut, she ran her hands over his head, holding him close. Sam reached down and adjusted her hips so that his cock nestled right between her folds. As her need grew, moisture pooled. With her climax brimming, Lexi could barely hold on.

*Bite his neck,* her wolf urged. *Mate with him.*

*Later.* She didn't need to be arguing with her wolf.

Lexi glided back and forth over his cock, and they both groaned. Sam gripped her hips as he closed his eyes and laid his head back against the couch seemingly lost to the sensation.

Suddenly, Lexi slipped off his lap then knelt on the floor between his legs. She bent over, close to his cock. When she looked up, Sam's gaze connected with hers and she grinned. "My turn to taste you."

She wrapped her hand around his erection, and then ran her tongue up his length and around the pulsing dark red head of his cock.

Sam's body shot off navy blue sparks, morphing into a blue halo around his body. "Holy shit," he gasped.

As a soldier, he should be able to withstand all kinds of torture, though she hoped this would be a wonderful kind of anguish.

Sam clasped her shoulder. "That feels so fucking good."

Wait until she sucked on him hard. With one hand, she held his rigid length upright and with the other, she cupped his balls. Heat seeped through her as she lightly circled the top of his cock again. Squeezing his hard shaft, she pumped her hand up then down. With each stroke, he moaned louder and louder. Finally, Sam grabbed her hair and tugged. When his hot cum tinged her tongue, it was her signal to take him.

Keeping her gaze on his lust-filled face, she crawled onto his lap again. "Ready?" she asked.

"More than you can know."

Widening her legs, she lifted up and took hold of his cock. Taking aim, she slowly sank down on him. Each delicious inch stretched her wide, and the slight pain only added to the exciting experience.

Leaning over, Lexi kissed him, but this time she kept her lips soft, protecting him from her sharpened teeth. She moved her tongue slowly, exploring what he had to offer. Sam moaned then grabbed her hips and thrust upward, sending her spiraling. She increased her rhythm, both with her hips and with her tongue.

Staying inside her, Sam wrapped his arms around her and stood. He moved to the end of the couch and then slipped out of her, forcing her to lower her feet to the floor. "Turn around and put your hands on the sofa arm."

Willing to do anything he asked, Lexi spread her legs wide. As soon as she bent over, he drove his big cock deep into her. Her spine tingled with erotic lust, and her heart pounded against her ribs.

With him now in control, he plunged deeper and harder. This time her wolf refused to be silent. Hair grew and nails sharpened. When he reached underneath her to twist and tug on her nipples, her world spun, and more bones cracked. Her arms glowed blue and her breaths turned rapid. Lexi lowered her head to draw in more air just as Sam's lips found her neck and sucked hard. That did her in.

"Lexi, I'm so close."

So was she. His cock expanded and stretched her even wider. Heat filled her from the inside, causing her own traitorous body to nearly explode.

*Please don't shift!* she warned her wolf.

His hands slipped to her waist and he plowed into her over and over again until she could no longer keep from coming. On the last thrust, a giant orgasm swooped in, and a second after her climax claimed her, his cock detonated.

She closed her eyes, but not before she caught sight of his body's glow growing larger. His dick continued to pulse as her orgasm slowly waned. Weak beyond belief, she dropped to her elbows and placed her head on her hands.

Sam put his forehead against her back, his heavy breathing cascading across her skin. Once they caught their breath, he placed a kiss between her shoulder blades. Sam pulled away and ran his hand down her spine. "I'll get something to clean us up with. Stay here."

It was all Lexi could do to get around the arm of the leather couch and flop down onto her back. She draped her arm up over her eyes as she let her body enjoy the satiated feeling. Drawers opened and water ran.

Sam returned. He chuckled. "Have you passed out on me?"

She lifted her arm and grinned. "Not yet, but I am getting close. I don't think I can move anything."

Sam gently cleaned her up and took care of himself as well. Tossing the cloth next to her jeans on the floor, he crawled onto the couch then lifted her, placing her on top of him as if she weighed nothing at all. She wrapped her arms around his neck and rested her head on his chest. This was where she needed to be.

VINEA WAS PISSED. Royally pissed. She paced in front of Justin and his men in their cramped, dingy hotel room. "You knew the deal," she said. "I find that little twerp for you, and you bring me Sam Pompley. What the hell happened?"

Justin glared at Don Diego, who straightened up. "You saw what happened," Diego said with way too much attitude. "We tried to grab Pompley, but he managed to shake us off."

She furrowed her brows and wished she could take them out

with a swipe of her hand, but she'd been stripped of most of her powers when she'd been tossed out the light realm all those years ago. Damn. "The blast wasn't anything more than smoke."

Diego shook his head. "The podium blew up, but he never came close enough for it to do much damage. He'd turned around and was heading back to the chick, so I had to detonate it then or not at all."

She supposed that was true. Vinea faced Justin. "And the girl; you didn't even get her, did you?"

"No, but that wasn't the plan. Once you do your thing with Sam, I'll waltz in and offer my sympathies for her loss. Lexi will come crawling back to Vermont where she belongs," Justin said.

He was on crack, but let him think whatever he wanted. "I don't care about the girl. I need you and your men to bring Pompley down." So she could do her thing. Vinea needed some of her powers restored, and stealing Sam's would be a great start. If she didn't, her days in the dark realm would be numbered.

"Don't you worry your pretty little head about it; I have a plan," Justin said.

She so wanted to shove a fist into his smug mouth, but she had to restrain herself. If anyone found out she was a goddess on a mission, heads would roll—namely hers. "See that you do. And don't take long."

"We won't."

Not able to stand being in the same room as these men, Vinea left. If they failed, she'd have to go to plan B, which involved using Devon McKinnon. But first, she wanted to try something on her own.

SAM WAS WORRIED about Lexi. After they drove back to the office, she didn't want to leave his side. She kept insisting that it was possible that Justin was targeting him. It didn't matter that it was to get to her. He told her he could take care of himself, but for some reason she didn't seem to be convinced. Sam could handle a punk like Kapok. Mind control was easy on the uninitiated.

Even after their intense and wonderful lovemaking, she was out of sorts, though it might be because she was afraid. "Would you like some company in your bed?" he asked.

Her eyes turned a pretty shade of amber. "Are you kidding? Of course, I want you to stay. My bed is huge."

Together, they headed down the secret passageway. As soon as they stepped into her suite, her step turned lighter. She spun around. "I need to shower," she said.

"Can I join you?"

"You sure? I'm warning you now that I can't be trusted to keep my hands to myself if we're naked."

Sam grinned. "I'm game. You wash my back, and I'll wash yours." He wiggled his eyebrows suggestively.

Lexi laughed. "Deal." As if they'd been together for years, she undressed quickly. "I'll warm up the water."

He hadn't seen her this animated since their wonderful snow-mobile adventure. Thinking of the outdoors, he vowed to take her into the wilderness again.

Sam rushed to undress. Washing with the bandage would be tricky, but he'd redo her handiwork if need be. Lexi was beautiful with her luscious curves and smooth skin. Sam couldn't help but soak in the sight of her as she stepped under the stream of the water. He followed right behind her, thinking being dirty in the shower could take on a whole new meaning.

He needed to reel those thoughts back. They'd already had some pretty intense sex, and he didn't want her to be sore tomorrow, but damn, it would take all of his control not to take her again.

"I can wash your hair," he said, craving the intimacy.

She handed him the shampoo and smiled. "Let me wet it first. Have you ever washed someone else's before?"

He hadn't. In fact, he hadn't even been in the same shower with a woman for a very long time. "No. Remember, until a few months ago, I've been overseas where fraternizing with the opposite sex was forbidden. I'm not saying it never happens, but I never did."

"I can't imagine what it was like being away from your family and not being able to hug them or talk with them every day. I'd go crazy being cooped up like that. Can you imagine if you and your mate were stationed together and yet you were forbidden to be together?"

Why was she bringing up mates? "Thankfully, that wasn't an issue."

As much as Sam wanted to ask if she thought he was her mate, he didn't really want to hear the answer, especially if she said no. Believing he wouldn't find his mate for a long time, he hadn't asked enough questions about how this fated mate stuff really worked. Only his grandfather had spoken of it when he was young.

Sam poured a bit of shampoo onto his palm and then rubbed it into her hair. It barely lathered. "You take more than me."

She laughed. "Well, I do have a lot more hair."

He hadn't been thinking, though who could blame him? Water was rushing over her perky tits, sending rivulets cascading between her legs. His mind kept jumping ahead to later. Lexi touched his arm, and he returned his focus to the task. After adding more shampoo, he was able to lather her hair. "Much better," he said.

She spun around. "I need to rinse." Facing him, she dipped her head back and let the water wash her hair clean. The temptation to lick her tits overwhelmed him, and sparks burst from every part of his body at that thought.

He cupped her breasts and lifted them. She squealed. "None of that. We're here to get the smoke off us," she said, but she didn't sound all that serious.

"You continue rinsing, and I'll play with these," he said.

She laughed as she shook her head. Once clean, she grabbed the liquid body wash and rubbed some on her arms. "You can do my back."

"I'd love to." He dribbled the soap over each shoulder. Unfortunately, it ran down her front, and his imagination turned wild. Before he had the chance to lather her tits, Lexi rubbed them slowly and teasingly. Sam closed his eyes and soaped up her back. Being this close to her and not thrusting his cock into her was driving him crazy. He wasn't sure if he could even handle her touching him right now. Hopefully, she'd become so desperate that they'd spend much of the night making love.

"Sam? I'm clean enough." Lexi laughed.

What the hell? As a soldier he never daydreamed. It could cost him his life. "Front good?"

She spun around. "I'm squeaky clean. Now, it's my turn." He thought she'd start with his hair, but he was wrong. She poured soap on his cock and pumped her fist up and down. Not only did his sparks shoot around the small shower space, but Lexi's did too. Before he could grab her hand to stop her, some of his cum spurted out. Because Lexi didn't react, she probably didn't notice.

He flipped around until his back was toward her. "I need my back worked on." Once more she did the unexpected. Lexi polished his rear to a shine. "You're asking for trouble, you know that?"

"Am I?" She rubbed her hands up and down his back, and he began to glow. This wasn't good. "I can see you appreciate my technique," she said.

Sam swung around. "I more than just appreciate it."

He pressed her against the back wall and kissed her until he was unable to hold back any longer. His need outstripped his desire to keep his distance.

After rinsing, he turned off the shower then led Lexi onto the bath mat. Without saying a word, he rubbed her down, hoping that by not touching her directly he'd calm down. His plan failed. With each drag of the terry cloth, her moans grew louder, and her sparks turned a deeper blue, sending his libido sky high.

Not caring that he hadn't dried off yet, he lifted her up and carried her toward the bedroom.

"You're all wet." Her complaint didn't ring true as her eyes turned pure amber.

"The better to slip into you, girl."

Lexi laughed and a bit more of his heart was lost to her.

# Chapter Twelve

FOR MUCH OF the next day, Sam tried not to wander into the reception area, recognizing that his ability to keep from ravishing her was growing weaker by the day. Having the safe room a few feet away didn't help either.

A knock sounded on his office door, and Devon popped in. "What's up?" Sam asked.

"I went to the restaurant to speak with Jacob, your waiter, who you suspected might be one of Kapok's men."

Sam sat up straighter. "Yes, what did you learn?"

"He wasn't there."

"Aren't they open for business yet?" Except for the blown up podium, it would be an easy cleanup. The odor from the smoke bomb would have aired out in a matter of hours. It wasn't like smoke from a fire.

"They opened for lunch today. According to the manager, the smoke cleared out rather quickly. Someone by the name of Brian Stanley said he could build a makeshift stand for them in a couple of days, so all's good."

That was nice of Jillian's mate to offer. "Was this Jacob guy supposed to work today?"

"Yes. Both shifts, but he was a no show. And yes, I asked for his address, but when I arrived, the address didn't exist. I asked around, but no one remembered ever seeing him."

"That gives some credence to the idea that he works for Kapok.

What about the hostess? Did she get an ID on the woman?"

"The hostess said no one approached her."

Damn. "So this waiter must have been working under someone else's orders."

"It's possible. If you want me to follow up on anything, let me know."

"Thanks." Devon took off, and Sam returned to his deskwork, his mind spinning. He would give it a day or two to see if the guy showed up at work, and then he'd investigate more fully.

Before he had the chance to click a key on his computer, his cell rang. It was his sister! She rarely called during business hours. "Hey, Teagan."

"Hey there. Rumor has it you've found your mate!"

His heart sputtered. "Who told you that?" He hadn't meant for the anger to sneak out, but between the blast and the frustration at not finding any clues, he was at his wits end.

"Oh, you know what it's like in our close-knit community. Connor might have mentioned it to Rye who in turn spilled the beans to Izzy, who mentioned it to Missy, who just happened to tell me."

He had to laugh. That was probably quite accurate. "I can't be positive, but because I can't get into Lexi's head at all, it just might mean she is my mate. At least that's what Grandpa Pompley told me years ago." He wasn't going to tell his sister the details about how hard it was to keep away from Lexi. "But please don't say anything to her. We haven't even discussed it yet."

"Mum's the word. I called because we want to meet her."

*We?* "As in you and Izzy?"

"Those and a few more."

"That's great, but until this crazy man who's after her is caught. I don't want to let her out of my sight," Sam said.

"Relax! There will be a ton of us to protect her. If Elana can't shift and deal with the pesky wolves, then Izzy can throw fire at them, though if Anna changed into her tiger form, no one would survive. Hell, I can always Taser one or two. I'm getting quite good with my new skills."

"I need to remember not to piss you off." She laughed. If Jackson's mate was going to be there, she could easily become invisible and attack several wolves at once. Jackson claimed that when four wolves had jumped him, the Changelings had no idea what was happening. Ainsley was that good. "Fine, but don't fill her head with too much stuff. The poor girl is still in shock from everything. I'll ask Lexi to see if she's up for it. What day and time?"

"Tomorrow evening at six thirty at Rye's house. We'll supply everything. If you drive her there, one of us can take her back to the office when we're done."

He smiled. "I'll let you know. And thanks." Sam placed his phone on the table, pleased that his sister had reached out. If Lexi had some friends, and was made welcome, she might consider staying when this was over.

He pushed back his chair and headed out to tell her, figuring she'd be excited to go if only to get away from the office. Sam could have called or texted her, but he wanted to see her in person. Man, did he have it bad.

As he passed through the main room, Connor was fixing some coffee. Sam debated asking him what right he had to blab that Sam and Lexi were an item, but in the end, it was probably for the best. Sam would have to let everyone know eventually. When he would broach the topic to Lexi about them being mates, he didn't know.

Sam stepped into the reception area and spotted Lexi hunched over her computer. The moment she caught sight of him, she sat up. "Hey! Any news about Jacob or his mystery woman?"

"No." He told her that Devon had been unable to find their waiter. "Apparently, Jacob gave a bogus address and is nowhere to be found."

"It doesn't matter. Justin won't give up, and when he makes his move, we'll get him."

Sam didn't like the, *we* part. He wanted Lexi as far from Kapok as possible at all times. "My sister, Teagan, called and wants to meet you."

"Really? I'd love that. Is she coming here?"

He explained about the dinner at Rye's place. "There's enough magic and shifter power to take out anyone. Plus, I'm sure that Rye will be somewhere in the background." Sam would speak with him before the party to make sure. "You'll be as safe there as you would here with me. Maybe more so."

She grinned. "Sounds wonderful. I can get all the dirt on you."

Other than when he was growing up, he doubted Teagan knew all that much about him. "While I have nothing to hide, don't listen to what any of those women say. They're all lies—unless it's good stuff."

She laughed. "I'll look forward to meeting them all." He told her when it was and that he'd be driving her, but that one or more of the women would return her to the office.

Connor's voice boomed in the background, calling his name. "Hey, I gotta go." Sam glanced around, and when he didn't hear anyone approach, he leaned over and kissed her.

That one little taste might have been a mistake, because his body practically glowed neon blue.

LEXI COULDN'T BELIEVE the time had finally come to meet Sam's sister and her friends. She was so looking forward to getting out and socializing. Other than the men at McKinnon and Associates, she hadn't seen another friendly face.

Because she had an hour break between the end of her workday and the party, she wanted to shower and then put on some makeup. Sam had picked up a few things for her at the store, understanding that she'd feel more like herself if she had some lipstick and blush.

Once she dressed in her jeans and a nice dark plum sweater, she went in search of Sam.

When she stepped into his office, he glanced up and placed the pencil he'd been using on his desk. "You ready?" he asked.

"Yup." She lifted the arm holding her coat to show him she had everything she needed.

Even though she'd never met these women, Lexi was thrilled to have some downtime where she wouldn't have to think about Justin and what his next move might be. Not being surrounded by testosterone would be a nice change too. Back in Vermont, she had a few good friends, but not a ton. Meeting so many others, especially who were either a shifter or Wendayan, or even a mix was going to be so much fun.

Sam grabbed his keys and coat. "Let's go. By the way, you look really hot in that sweater."

She grinned. "Maybe you can show me how much later on."

He laughed. "You have a one track mind. Then again, so do I." He winked, and her heart lurched.

The air outside, while cold, didn't have the usual bite to it, for which she was thankful. The sky was clear and the moon half full.

They both piled into his truck. "I'll give you the quick rundown on who's likely to be there," Sam said. "By the way, the party is at Ryerson McKinnon's house."

"He's Alpha of the shifter Clan and Connor and Devon's brother. That much I know."

"You've been paying attention. Good. His mate, Izzy, is a very powerful Wendayan despite having lost some of her powers after she mated with Rye. Izzy can control wind, water, earth, and fire."

Wow. "If she's mated to the Alpha, she must be even more powerful now."

"She is. Being able to shift has really added to her strengths. Her sister is Missy, and she's unattached. She's pure Wendayan." He explained about her healing abilities. "Missy works with Teagan at the Crystal Winds Spa. My sister used to have a lot of bad premonitions until she mated with Kip. Since then, her outlook has improved, and now she can see good things too—like Elana's pregnancy."

Lexi liked hearing success stories like that. "I figured it would be hard to remember who was who, so I studied the chart you made for me. I remember that Elana is mated to Kalan, Jackson's brother."

He smiled. "You're good."

"You said my life depended on knowing this information."

"You're right."

"Who else will be there?" she asked.

"Besides Izzy, Missy, my sister, and Elana, there's Anna, who is Elana's assistant at the flower shop. She's mated to Kalan's partner, Dalton."

Both were on the list Sam had given her. "She was human and was mated to Dalton, who is Jillian's brother. All of them can move fast."

"Wow. You're a quick learner. I think that's all, but what do I know? I'm not in town often enough to see them on a regular basis, but Connor and Rye keep me updated."

"It's so nice of your sister to invite me. People don't usually throw parties for strangers."

"They are nice, but I suspect their true intention is to grill you on your relationship with me. I haven't told Teagan much, so you can make up anything you see fit."

"I might be discreet, or I might not be. When girls get together, there's no telling what we might say."

Sam groaned, and Lexi inwardly chuckled. Keeping a man off balance was a good thing. He turned into a housing complex and then stopped in front of a house with several cars parked in front. "Here we are. Someone will drive you home, but if you'd rather have me pick you up, just call."

He was so sweet. "Don't worry about me. Given the power in that house, we can take down an army of wolves." She leaned over and kissed him. Even that small contact caused sparks to fly and her wolf to wake up. "I better go before we have sex in the backseat of your truck—which by the way, I've never done."

He grinned. "I'll add it to our bucket list."

She laughed then pushed open the car door. With the house light blazing, and the sidewalk shoveled clear of snow, it was easy to reach the front entrance. After one knock, the door opened, and a sea of eager eyes greeted her. She held out her hand. "Hi, I'm Lexi."

"I'm Izzy." She was very tall with long red hair and was stunningly beautiful. Izzy waved to Sam then shut the front door. "I'm Rye's mate."

"Nice to meet you."

A strong wave of shifter signatures filled the room. Supposedly, everyone except for Missy and Teagan was a shifter, either from birth or because of mating. Each of the women introduced themselves, but one name didn't sound familiar. "Blair, how are you connected to these women?" Lexi pulled out the piece of paper with the tree of who was who on it and held it up. "Sam made me this." She handed it to her.

Blair, who was also tall, studied the chart. "You can pencil me in here. I'm Jackson's sister."

"Oh!" She wondered how that had escaped Sam's attention.

The girls scooted over and Lexi sat between Anna and Ainsley on the sofa.

Blair shook her head. "I haven't contributed directly to McKinnon and Associates, so I can see why he forgot me."

"Help yourself to the wine," Izzy said. "We'll eat shortly. Tell us about yourself."

Lexi had a million questions for them, but it might make more sense if these women knew her better. Because she didn't want to hide anything, she started with how her dad had tried to sell her. "I know my father had drinking and gambling problems, but I never thought he'd stoop that low."

The group gasped. "I thought my stepfather was bad," Ainsley said. "Since both parents are Changelings, they merely ignored me, though for the right amount of money, I bet my dad would have sold me." Everyone chuckled. Lexi needed to find out more about these evil beings. Sam had filled her in but not completely.

Izzy cut in. "I don't know about your dad, Ainsley, but your brother was horrible enough to sell you." She turned to Lexi. "Ainsley's brother tried to kidnap me." She winked. "Try being the operative word."

Ainsley nodded. "Owen was always too full of himself, which in the end was his downfall. I'm glad Rye took him out. Speaking of alpha males, I trust Sam told you about the evil Changelings?"

"He gave me a brief rundown. I'm glad I'm going against an ordinary werewolf and not battling one of them."

Ainsley smiled. "Very true. I was one, but thanks to the wonderful people of Silver Lake, I was able to be cleansed and am now Changeling free." The smile was directed at Izzy, which implied she was involved. "But go ahead with your story."

Lexi would have to find out about her interesting tale later. "After Bill—that's my dad—told me about the imminent sale, I got the hell out of Dodge."

Jillian sighed. "I feel your pain. I had to run away too."

"What happened?"

"A cop shot and killed my former roommate who'd flown in for a bachelorette party." Now it was Lexi's turn to suck in a big breath.

"You witnessed a murder? What did you do?"

"I only saw the aftermath, but I knew who'd killed my friend. Fearing he'd come back for me, I kind of freaked. Even though it was two in the morning, I packed a bag and hopped on a plane from California to come here. I rented a car and ran straight to my big brother, Dalton."

"You were lucky you had someone. I only stopped here because I ran out of gas." Wanting full disclosure, she told them how Sam and Connor had found her eating out of the trash bin. She told them she was in her wolf form at the time.

"Eww," Anna said, "though if I'd been that hungry, who knows what I might have done."

Izzy stood. "Speaking of hungry, how about we grab a bite to eat and then hear the rest of Lexi's story?"

"Don't you have an announcement to make?" Missy said.

Izzy's face turned pink. "I was waiting until I could tell all of you at once. I guess this is as good a time as ever."

"Tell us!" Jillian practically shouted with great enthusiasm.

"Rye and I are expecting our first child in August."

Several of the women shrieked while others clapped. Eventually, they all jumped up and hugged her. Anna placed a hand on her own protruding belly, and Lexi leaned over. "When are you due?"

"June. Dalton and I are so excited. I can't wait until our child shifts. I just love kittens."

Lexi tried to remember what species she was. "You're a white tiger, right?"

"Yes."

"Come on, everyone. Eat up," Elana said.

The group of ladies crowded around the buffet that contained platters of cold cuts, three different types of salads, and four casseroles. Lexi wanted to sample everything, so she took some of each. "This is amazing. Thank you for this," she said to both Izzy and Elana who were next to her.

Izzy smiled. "We want to start a tradition of having a get together every month or two where we each bring a dish."

"Sounds wonderful," she said, though she wasn't sure if she'd still be there in a few months.

After working her way around the table, Lexi took her plate back to the living room.

Elana sipped her wine. "Lexi, when you're done eating, please finish your story. I'm fascinated how your auspicious visit in a dumpster had you ending up sitting here. I thought Kalan told me there was some guy after you."

"Yes. The man who my dad owed money to." She then explained how after she arrived in Silver Lake, Connor and his team asked Devon to check out Justin Kapok. "My father warned me that Justin was determined to mate with me and would come after me no matter what. To find more information on him, Devon flew up to Vermont. He found him. Somehow Devon learned that Justin and his crew were headed to Silver Lake to find me."

Izzy shook her head. "I know the feeling of being stalked. The worst part is the wait."

"You can say that again." Now that she had this powerhouse of knowledge in front of her, she wanted to take advantage of it. "The only good thing to come of all this is that I met Sam. I will admit he fascinates me. What can you tell me about him?" Naturally, her gaze drifted to Teagan.

"You might know him better than I do since he's been overseas for so long. Even though he's back home, he works a lot. I know that growing up, he was fun to be with, until Dad decided to embrace all things paranormal. Our father kind of changed his focus in life from us kids to teaching others. It took me years to realize that I couldn't let what my parents said or did affect me now."

"I feel the same way," Lexi said. "When my mom was alive, my life was good. Even Bill was more or less happy. I have an older brother who is great, but he had his own life—playing sports, dating, and being with friends. A few years ago Mom became ill, and when she died, Bill turned inward. Ronan, my brother, distanced himself too. He said he just couldn't bring himself to babysit our father. So now I'm on my own."

Most in the group nodded. Blair looked around. "I'm so sorry. I feel lucky that I have great parents, but Elana and Anna had a raw deal, and Jillian's dad was murdered when she was six."

One by one, the women told their stories about how they all became friends. Lexi had never been in a room where such strength and affection existed in one place before. "You've all led such interesting, or maybe I should say, trying and brave lives; from being stalked, to being beaten and kidnapped, and to sneaking into a Changeling's house, not to mention seeing your good friend after she was killed, and then taking down the killer. Wow. You guys rock."

"If I may speak for all of us," Izzy said, "we are better women because of it. Without Ainsley's stepbrother wanting me as his mate, I never would have met Rye."

Elana nodded. "If the Changelings hadn't wanted the red onyx my parents had, I never would have ended up with Kalan."

Lexi chuckled. "I guess I belong in that club too. If my father hadn't tried to sell me to Justin Kapok, I wouldn't have found Sam."

The buzzing in the room picked up again as they all discussed their darkest moments and how those times turned out to be the best thing in their lives. But Lexi hoped she wouldn't have to go through that kind of angst again.

For the next hour and a half the women chatted about their jobs, as well as their hopes and dreams. Lexi was particularly interested in where Izzy taught. She asked if there were any openings.

"We don't have any math positions now, but come Sept, I'll need someone to teach chemistry for me when I go on maternity leave."

Lexi shook her head. "I took Chem, but I don't know it well enough to teach it."

"I understand. I thought I'd mention it. If I hear of any math openings, I'll let you know. Our school is expanding all the time."

How nice was that? "Thank you."

A shifter signature entered the room, and Lexi turned around. A tall, very good-looking man entered, his smile aimed directly at Izzy. He must be Rye. His gaze swung around toward Lexi. He approached then held out his hand. "I'm Rye. Nice to meet you."

She'd never met an Alpha before, and he looked like the perfect one too. "I'm Lexi Laramie."

He smiled at her then faced the crowd. "My mate is feeling a bit tired ladies."

It took a moment for Lexi to remember that Rye could sense everything about Izzy. The rest of the women jumped up and collected the dishes they'd brought. Lexi helped where she could. She then walked around to each of the women saying how much she'd enjoyed meeting them.

Rye came over to her. "I'll be happy to drive you home."

As wonderful as it had been to meet the women, she would be happy to see Sam again. "I'd appreciate it."

# Chapter Thirteen

THE NEXT FEW days were rather hectic, and Lexi almost stopped thinking about Justin. She could only hope that if he had come to Silver Lake, he was no longer here. She just wished she could find out for certain.

Lexi snapped her fingers. Ronan might be able to find out. Picking up the burner phone Sam had given her, she called her brother.

He answered on the third ring. Most likely he was in his car tracking someone. "Ronan Laramie."

"Ronan, it's me." The sound of an engine filled the background.

"Lex? Hey, how's it going? You okay?"

"I guess. Listen, I need a favor." She described how it had been more than a week since Justin Kapok had theoretically left Vermont for Tennessee. "No one's seen him. Either he never planned to come here, or he came here, and when he couldn't find me, he trucked back up to Vermont."

"Would you like me to ask around?"

"That would be great. You can find him, right?"

"I can find anyone. It's all a matter of time. I'll look into it and contact you if I learn anything."

"You're the best. I want to get my life back, and I can't if I'm not allowed to leave this building."

"I hear ya," he said. "It's got to be better than Dad's trailer though."

"Very true." She was disgusted with what Bill had done and

didn't want him causing trouble for her brother now that she had left. "Is he harassing you for money?"

"I drive by every few days to make sure he's alive, but I'm not giving him any money. He'll just drink it or gamble it away."

"I know." A horn blared on Ronan's end. "I won't keep you, but thanks for looking."

"Sure thing."

When she disconnected, Lexi was both relieved and a little depressed. She missed Ronan. He always had been a steadying force in her life. Adding to her discontent today had been the fact that Sam had been called out on a case. While it was a surveillance job, she missed him being at the office. She debated calling him, but with her luck, he'd be sneaking around the property when his cell rang and get caught.

Needing a break from working on her spreadsheets, she played solitaire on her computer. Before she'd completed the first game, the office phone rang. "McKinnon and Associates. How may I help you?"

"Lexi, it's Sam."

Her pulse sped up at just hearing his voice. "What's up?"

"It was the stupidest thing. I was on my way back to the office when I hit a patch of ice. The truck skidded, and I slammed into a tree."

Her heart jumped to her throat. "Are you okay?"

"I'm fine, but the truck's not. Can you pick me up?"

"Sure. Where are you?" He gave her detailed instructions. "I'll leave right now."

She disconnected and then rushed through the main room to the hallway. She hadn't even reached the door that led to her safe room when she realized she didn't have the keys to her car. Sam had them. He'd forgotten to give them back the night he looked for the tracker on her car—or else he didn't want her sneaking off and running into Justin. She supposed she could get a cab, but it would be faster if Devon, Connor, or Jackson could drive her.

Since she was closest to Devon's office, she knocked on his door and entered. He jumped up. "What's wrong?"

How could he tell something was wrong? When she glanced down at her hands, they were shaking. "Sam just called and said he was in a car wreck."

"Oh fuck. Is he okay?"

"Yes, but his truck isn't. He asked that I come get him, only I realized that I don't have my keys. Do you think you could pick him up?"

Devon's brows pinched as he ran a hand over his head. "Are you sure he asked that you come get him? Sam has been very adamant about you not going anywhere?"

"I know, but when he asked, I figured he thought it must be safe."

"And you're sure it was Sam."

Lexi planted a hand on her hip. "I'm very good with voice recognition. It was Sam."

"Okay, okay. Let me call him and see if he just needs help or if he wants me to call a tow truck."

She didn't understand why Devon was not rushing out to help his friend, but without a car, she didn't have much choice. He picked up his phone and dialed Sam. "Hey, are you okay? Lexi said you just called and told her you'd been in a wreck. Let me put you on speaker." He pressed the button. "Go ahead."

"I didn't call Lexi," Sam said. "What's going on?"

Her legs weakened, and she dropped down onto the chair in front of his desk. She leaned close to the phone. "I just spoke to you," she said.

"Hon, I didn't call you. Tell me exactly what was said."

She tried to remember every detail. "Are you saying someone impersonated your voice?" How was that possible?

"I don't know, but there are voice synthesizers that might fool you. It couldn't be the Changelings. The red moon was over a week ago. Might it have been Justin?"

Justin had a slight northern accent. "I can't be sure."

"Devon," Sam said. "How about calling Kalan and asking if he and Dalton can head out to the supposed crash site? I'll meet them there."

"I don't think you should go," Devon said. "It might be a trap to put you out of commission so they can get to Lexi."

"Damn, you may be right." Sam said. "Fine. Stay with Lexi until I get there."

Her heart swelled. Sam would always be there for her. While some members of her Clan in Vermont might not be faithful, Sam sure seemed to be.

"I'll call Kalan right now," Devon said. He then disconnected. "I don't know what to tell you, Lexi, but someone is out to get either you or Sam."

She slumped in her seat. "This sucks." Drawing on all her inner strength, she stood to leave.

"If you want to head out front, that's okay, but don't let anyone in, no matter who it is. If you think they are legit, come get me."

"Okay." Lexi headed back to her seat, hoping Sam would get there soon.

VINEA WAS LIVID. How had her plan gone so wrong? That bitch Lexi was either smart or else she didn't care for Sam like Vinea had thought. When the cop car rolled up, instead of Lexi's Toyota, Vinea assumed they'd stopped because of the accident.

She did get some satisfaction when they ran the plates and were confused by the fact they belonged to Sam. Eventually, they'd figure out this truck had been stolen from the local car dealership lot, and Sam's plates had been exchanged, but for now they were making calls and scrambling for evidence. She had to laugh at their attempt to find fingerprints. Like she'd leave any?

With her carefully placed plan foiled, she needed a new tactic, one that involved Devon McKinnon. How much fun would it be to steal Sam's magic, and then have Devon be blamed for it? Her plan was for Justin and his men to incapacitate Sam first. With him nearly comatose, she'd swoop in and take his magic. She could almost feel his abilities soaring through her body now.

It was time to have a little powwow with Justin and his mates. They had a plan ready, or so they said, and she needed to hurry them along. One way or the other, Sam's magic would be hers soon.

WHEN SAM ARRIVED at the office, he was jittery and angry. Lexi had never seen him like this. "Are you sure you're okay?" she asked as she followed him into the main room.

"I'm worried."

She was worried too. "I'm still confused about what happened. Is your car okay?"

"Yes, it is, but I checked with the local police; someone stole my plates and then replaced them with some other vehicle's plates."

Connor and Devon came in the main room from the hallway, along with Jackson. They each filled up their cups. "Let's head to the auditorium," Connor said.

In silence, she and Sam followed. A large table sat on a raised platform at one end. It faced a U-shaped group of seats. Jackson moved to the front and faced them.

"I've spoken with Kalan, and here is what we have." He pulled up a slide that listed facts. "First, the car was stolen from Lander's Motors sometime last night. Kalan will ask for the surveillance to see if we can see who did the stealing. Secondly, the plates were Sam's."

Sam blew out a breath. "I have to be honest. I haven't looked at my plates in quite a while. They could have been stolen a week ago for all I know."

Jackson nodded. "To bring Lexi up to speed, every phone call that comes into this office is recorded. I quickly compared the voice to that of Sam's. I'll have to study it more carefully, but with the quick listen I did, it sounded like a match."

"How is that possible?" Sam asked. "I did not make that call. The fact my truck wasn't in the accident should prove that. Besides, I was—"

Jackson held up his hand. "Easy there. No one is accusing you of anything. Whoever called is sophisticated. I'll have to do more research, but right now I'm not aware of anything that can perfectly replicate a voice, but clearly this person possesses it. When I find out where it is manufactured, I might buy one." A few of the men chuckled.

"So what are you saying?" Connor asked. "We're dealing with someone who is highly sophisticated."

"Or this person has a magical talent, unlike anything we've seen before."

Damn.

"I don't see Justin as being this sophisticated" Lexi piped up. "However, he's wealthy; really wealthy. Maybe he has access to some prototype technology."

"For the right price, anything is possible," Jackson said.

"It would explain a lot," Connor said.

"I've done some research on him and watched Kapok in action," Devon chimed in. "He likes to get his power from smooth talking. It's possible he learned about this device while gambling. Hell, he might have won it in a game of chance."

Jackson nodded. "It's possible, though at first I thought the Changelings might be involved somehow, but their red moon has past."

"Someone touched me at the restaurant, but that was days ago," Sam said. "Otherwise, I would have suggested a Changeling was trying to become me."

Jackson shook his head. "I don't think the Changelings are involved. I'll speak with Ainsley to see if she's picked up any chatter, but we should focus on Kapok and his men for right now."

"Did you check our surveillance footage to see who stole my plate?" Sam said. "Admittedly, the theft could have occurred when I was parked by the church last Sunday, when I was having dinner at the Lake Steakhouse, or at my house. Shit. We're never going to get this guy are we?"

Lexi rubbed Sam's arm. He seemed more anxious than she was to get Justin.

"We are," Connor said. "We just need to be patient."

Lexi raised her hand. "I've mentioned this before, but I'm willing to walk up and down Main Street and window shop, trying to draw Justin out in the open. You could glue tracking devices all over my body, along with a wire. Hell, Jackson could fly his drone overhead. You said you have a ton of shifters in the Clan who are willing to help, right?" She spoke as quickly as possible in hopes they would understand the lengths she was willing to go to in order capture this guy.

"Not going to happen," Sam said. Steel laced his tone.

"Sorry, Lexi," Connor chimed in. "We don't put our clients in jeopardy like that."

Well shit. She'd tried this tact three times, and she'd been shot down each time. With all the glares coming her way, she wasn't going to win—ever, but she'd figure out something. "Fine. I'll hole up here, but there has to be something we can do."

Sam rubbed her hand. "Justin will make a mistake, and when he does, we'll get him."

"In the meantime, I'm assigning Devon to this case full time," Connor said. "He'll be coordinating things. I don't think we anticipated your stalker would take your capture to this extreme. We need to up our game."

That worked for her.

# Chapter Fourteen

V INEA'S MEETING WITH Justin and his men had gone better than planned. They decided—or rather she decided—that she would monitor Sam and Lexi's movements to learn when those two planned to be in the open. Once she had the time and location, Justin and his men would incapacitate Sam for her. The victory would be so sweet—and long overdue—when she could bend the mind of others.

Donning slim jeans, a red body-hugging long sleeve jersey that showed just the right amount of cleavage, and her zippered knee high boots, she swiped a hand across her torso, and suddenly, a down jacket hugged her body. She loved magic.

Next stop? McKinnon and Associates. Given the high level of security in the place, it would take some sweet-talking to get past the front door, but once in, she was confident she could convince Devon to do her bidding. She could always just appear in his office, but then he'd know she was no ordinary woman.

First thing she'd need was a car. Because acquiring the same model of truck that Sam drove had been so easy, she decided to try again, only this time, it would be some older model car. She wasn't without all of her magic, and what little she did possess, she'd use to her advantage.

Once Vinea arrived at the McKinnon office in a soccer-mom car that she'd changed from white to gray with another swipe of her hand, she fished out the business card Devon had given her and pranced up the front steps. When she pressed the bell, Lexi answered and asked what she was there for.

Vinea used her distressed-female voice. "I need to speak with Devon McKinnon." She held up the business card he'd given her in front of the overhead camera.

"Just a moment please."

Vinea inwardly smiled. She could picture Lexi rushing to find him. When he identified her, Vinea would be on her way to getting her life back.

"Vinea?" Devon's rich voice sounded over the intercom, and something inside her sizzled. She pushed aside that unwanted and unidentifiable feeling. Ever since she'd first met him, her reaction to him had pissed her off. She felt unbalanced and out of control, something that had never happened before. When she'd danced with Justin, nothing like that had occurred. She would have remembered.

"Yes, it's me. I need your help again. You said to call if I needed you." Okay, this wasn't exactly a phone call, but from the way he'd looked at her at both the bar and later the restaurant back in Vermont, he had appeared interested in her.

The door clicked and Devon appeared. "Come in."

Well, that was easy.

He placed a hand on her back as if they'd already been intimate, and the heat from his palm nearly burned her. She jerked, literally. What was up with that?

"Tell me what you need," Devon said as he led her past Lexi, through a large oak door, and into a room with a large table at one end.

She had hoped for the confines of his office, but he probably didn't consider her a client since she wasn't a paying customer. "I found Justin Kapok."

His body stiffened, and she could see his teeth elongate. Hell, he seemed ready to go into battle. "Where is he?" Devon asked with gritted teeth.

"Someplace west of here." Actually, he was holed up in a seedy motel in the next town over.

"Listen, Vinea. This guy is dangerous. He's made threats against another woman. I don't want you going anywhere near him."

She waved a hand. "Justin won't hurt me."

"You can't know that. He's already proven that he can't be trusted. I don't want your death on my conscience."

For one, she couldn't die, and secondly, Justin wasn't capable of harming her, but she'd keep those two facts to herself. Devon's rather intense reaction wasn't something she had anticipated, but she could use it to her advantage.

She'd practiced what she had to say, but now that she was in front of him, the words weren't forming. "You're right. He is someone to be careful of. That's why I need to borrow some surveillance equipment from you."

"May I ask why? And please don't say you want to plant a listening device on him."

"Would that be so bad?"

Devon stabbed a hand through his hair. "He's a criminal and doesn't seem to have a conscience about who he hurts. How about telling me where he is and I'll retrieve your luggage."

She so didn't need him to be a macho man right now. "I'd rather do this myself."

Besides, Justin didn't have anything of hers. Devon's eyes darkened, and his fingers curled tighter around his cup. The tiniest molecule of guilt at the lie edged into her. Why had that happened? She never felt guilt over anything. Vinea sat up straighter, unhappy with that bit of weakness.

"No."

This wasn't going as planned. "Look, Justin trusts me. I can get in and get out before he knows anything. If you can lend me something then show me how to use it, I promise to tell you what he says and where he is."

"How will this help you get your stuff back?"

She shook her head then tilted it, pretending he was dense. "I'll know when his room is empty. I'll sneak in, grab my stuff, and then get the hell out of there. You'll get your gear back, and all will be good."

"It's too dangerous. It's not like you're a trained professional."

She was so much more than that. She had enough powers to stop that merry band of men. "I'll be careful."

"My men and I can plant the devices for you without him finding out. When we know they are gone, we'll search for your lost luggage."

If Devon was able to keep tabs on Justin, he and his team would learn what they planned to do to Sam, and Vinea couldn't let that happen. "No. If I get caught, I can just laugh it off."

"And I'll lose my equipment."

There was that. "I'd buy some myself if I knew what to buy and if I had money."

As Devon studied her, Vinea tried to look as distraught as possible. He pushed back his chair and a rush of satisfaction flowed through her. "Wait here."

Yes! That was a close call. What was it about this man that bothered her so? It shouldn't matter, but it had been ages since she'd felt anything other than disgust and hate for people.

While she waited, Vinea glanced around at this large room, impressed with the upscale facilities. Justin, who'd bragged about his material possessions, would never have digs this nice.

Devon returned, carrying a small box that he placed in front of her. "This is all I can spare. It's outdated, but it will get the job done. However, at the first hint of trouble, I want you to call me. I can have my men there in a heartbeat."

"I will. I promise."

She removed the lid. Eight small listening devices were seated in gray foam. "This is perfect."

"Let me show you how to use them." He went through a thorough explanation of where and how to place the devices.

"Thank you!" Devon smiled and her heart fluttered. While she'd never been sick in her life, the indoor air quality in the room must be super bad to make her pulse soar.

"You'll need this." He placed another box on the table. "Record what they say on this."

She smiled. "As soon as I get my stuff back, I'll return everything. I won't erase anything. You can hear what those motherfuckers say. I want to prove they are thieves."

The pulse in Devon's neck beat harder. Clearly, this was what he wanted.

"I'd like nothing more than to nail them. Where are you staying?" he asked.

"At a friend of my sister's." She was rather pleased with herself at how the lies kept flowing off her tongue.

She would have said she was sleeping in her car, if she thought he'd offer to let her stay with him, but Vinea had already learned he was at his folks' place. Apparently, his presence in Silver Lake was only temporary since he ran an office in Pennsylvania.

"Please don't do anything rash. If you're caught—"

"I won't. Don't worry about me, please." Sheesh. Overly protective men were so not her thing. Like she couldn't handle herself? Vinea stood and gathered her goodies. "I'll bring them back just as soon as I can."

Devon escorted her to the front. "Good luck."

She gave him her best smile and left. Today had been a good day.

SAM WAS ON his way back from his afternoon meeting with a potential client and was looking forward to seeing Lexi again. As much as he disliked leaving her for so long, she was in good hands. Both Devon and Jackson were in the office.

Just as Sam pulled his truck in front of the building, a tall woman with long dark auburn hair exited out of the front door. While he wasn't aware of what everyone was working on, he didn't remember anyone having a female client. Perhaps she was a new account.

Sam slipped from the front seat and headed inside. As he passed her, he nodded, but she didn't seem to even notice him. Focusing on seeing Lexi again, he pressed his finger against the scan, waited for the door to click, and then pulled it open.

There she was! Her hair was twisted on top of her head, and she seemed to be intent on something on the screen. Lexi must have sensed him however, because she looked up and smiled. Her eyes flashed amber for a moment before returning to a pretty brown, and his insides rumbled with joy. This last week or so had done wonders for her. Once Justin was caught, Sam suspected she'd blossom even more.

"Hi," he said as he closed the gap between them. Sam leaned over and kissed her briefly, even though he wanted more. Much more.

"How did your meeting go?" she asked.

"Good. I see we had a walk-in."

Lexi stilled for a moment. "Oh, the tall beautiful woman who just left?"

For a moment he thought she might be jealous, but Lexi didn't have to worry. "I guess so. I was so focused on seeing you that I barely noticed her."

Lexi's eyes lit up as she laughed. "You are so full of shit."

"Whatever. Who was she?"

Lexi lifted a shoulder. "Someone Devon knew. She stayed maybe fifteen minutes and then left. You'll have to ask him. I'm just the receptionist."

Sam planted his hands on the desk and leaned close. "You are so much more than a receptionist."

One brow rose. "That so?"

"Perhaps I'll have to convince you tonight just how special you are."

She grinned. "I can't wait."

Sam stood. "We'll discuss plans later. Right now, I'm going to check with Devon to see if he's made any progress on your case."

"Sounds good."

As Sam stepped into the main room, satisfaction rushed through him. Lexi had been jealous of that woman, implying she cared about him. Soon, he'd have to broach the topic of them being fated mates, though from the way her eyes had just turned amber, the same as when they made love, she might know they were meant to be together.

He knocked on Devon's door then entered. His friend looked up from his computer. "Hey, you're back."

Sam pulled up a chair and sat. "Yes. I got the lowdown on the man's wife, who he believes is having an affair. Rather standard stuff."

"Sounds simple."

"It should be. Say, I heard you had a visitor." He suspected it might be the same woman he'd befriended in Vermont.

"Lexi tell you?"

"Yes."

"It was Vinea, the woman I met in Vermont. She's still trying to get her stuff back from Justin. And she knows where he is."

Every muscle tensed. "What? You know where he is. Why are you sitting here?"

"It's not that easy." Devon pushed back his chair and stood. He strode in front of his desk and sat on the edge. "I don't know where he is. Vinea wouldn't tell me. I'm so mad at myself I could spit."

"You should have followed her. At the very least, you should have asked Jackson to use his drone."

"Fuck me. My brain stopped working the moment she walked in. I should have tailed her, but she's long gone now."

That was bad timing. "Start from the beginning." Sam clenched his fist. This was the first lead they'd gotten, and Devon let it slip through his fingers.

He told him how he'd let Vinea sweet-talk him into lending her some surveillance equipment.

"Are you kidding me? Did you tell her how dangerous Justin is?"

"I tried to warn her, but she said Justin has never harmed her."

"Harmed her? Hell, he took off with her luggage and left her stranded in Vermont. Does she think he's a nice guy?"

Devon huffed out a growl. "I don't know what she believes." He slapped the desk. "I'm such an idiot. I didn't even get her contact information. I just hope she calls so I can try to talk her out of it again. I think I was so excited to learn something about that scum that I let her convince me that she was capable of handling him."

Sam's pulse spiked. "Why wouldn't she tell you where he is?"

"She said that she didn't want us to muck things up or something like that. If she was caught, she'd laugh it off."

"Wait a minute. Are you buying her story? If she's that close to Kapok, why would he leave town without her in the first place?"

"I thought the same thing." He balled his fists. "She's in danger, and I let her walk into the lion's den."

"Did she say what Kapok was doing in town?"

He shook his head. "No, though to be honest, I'm not sure she knows any more than when she was in Vermont. Besides, Vinea is the queen of evasion. I agree there's something going on with her, but I can't put my finger on it—just that it isn't good."

Sam crossed his arms over his chest, trying to figure out what to say. Clearly, Devon had been blinded by her good looks if he parted with the listening devices—old or not. However, there was a slim chance everything would work out. "We need to find Justin. Did you forget he's a threat to Lexi? We need to get to him first."

"I know. I fucked up."

"How about I try to find her?"

"That would be great. If she does lead us to Kapok, we can do our own surveillance and learn what he's up to. Did you see what kind of car she drove?"

"It was a gray station wagon."

"She said she was staying with a friend of her sister's. It must be the friend's car or her sisters since Vinea took a bus down here—or so I think." Devon dropped his head back and sighed. "I can't believe I just handed over that equipment. It was like she put a spell on me."

Sam understood that feeling. From the moment he'd met Lexi, he'd been under her influence too. "Maybe she's your mate!"

Devon sat up and shot him a lethal glare. "I don't think so."

Many shifters seemed to deny their destiny, but he'd know if she were his mate. His body would be going crazy. "If you say so. All I know is that if we find Vinea, we will find Justin." Sam stood. "Is Jackson still here? I need him to check the camera feed and pull the plates."

"I think so."

"This is the first good lead we've had. I'll find out where her sister lives and take it from there. What's her last name?"

Devon's face turned red. "I never asked her."

"Some detective you are." Sam chuckled, but it was only to cut through the tension.

"Tell me about it. She's got to be a witch."

"Let's hope that's all she is."

Sam left and headed further down the hallway. He knocked on the partially open door, and Jackson motioned him in.

"If you have a sec, I need you to do something for me." Sam explained about Devon's guest and how Vinea claimed to know where Justin was staying.

"That's great. What do you need from me?" Jackson asked.

"Check the outdoor cameras and see if you can get a read on her plates."

Jackson smiled. "Come with me."

The two of them entered their monitoring room that looked as upscale as any military compound. Sam should learn how to use this equipment, but he was already so busy. Someday though. Besides Jackson was so damn good at it, he'd never catch up.

"Give me a sec," Jackson said as he typed something into the computer.

Seconds later, the front entrance camera lit up. Sam's car was already parked so this must be a live feed. "Can you back it up?"

"On it."

The image of Vinea driving in appeared on the screen, but she parked facing the front, preventing them from seeing the license plate. "Darn."

Jackson held up a hand. "Just wait. We have one camera across the way for this purpose." He typed more keys and sure enough a second image appeared. "Let me zoom in."

Sam couldn't see the plate well, but maybe Jackson could. "I can only make out the first three letters. The rest of the plate is caked with mud. I'll run this by Kalan and see what he comes up with."

"That's great. Let me know when you have something."

"Will do."

Sam left. While he'd been out and about all day, Lexi had been in the office, and he bet she'd enjoy getting out. Restaurants weren't an option for obvious reasons, and he didn't trust taking in a movie. But she might like cooking a meal together at his house. The small kitchen in the safe room wasn't conducive to a romantic affair. Also it would be nice to discuss with Lexi in private what he had found out about Justin Kapok.

Sam returned to his office to do a little bit of research on Vinea. An hour later, Jackson came to his office. "You won't believe what I found out about Vinea's car."

"What?"

"A car just like hers was stolen this morning from the Save A Lot grocery store. Only that one was white."

"What are you saying? That she had it painted gray?"

Jackson shrugged. "Without checking the VIN number, we can't be sure, but the woman whose car was taken described the decals on the bumper. They match Vinea's."

"Shit." That left out following her if they couldn't trace the car to her sister. He and Devon had been right to think something was off about her. "Are you going to break the news to Devon or should I?"

Jackson held up his hands. "I'm not saying a word."

"Coward."

Jackson smiled. "You got that right. I think he really likes her."

Sam had that impression too. This was one conversation he didn't want to have.

# Chapter Fifteen

L EXI WAS SUPER excited to go out with Sam. Not only would it give them some alone time, leaving her office cave would be a luxury. Yes, she would be careful. Ronan had called back and said that from what he could tell, Justin was still in Silver Lake. Even that news wouldn't put a damper on her night out with Sam. She just wished Justin would make his move.

She pictured the two of them cooking, flirting, laughing, and then having wild passionate sex. While they had made love in the room below, it wasn't the same as being with him in his house, which had been wonderful. One had become claustrophobic, the other romantic.

Sam came out with his coat in hand and smiled. "Ready for your outing?"

"More than ready." In fact, she had already retrieved her coat along with a small overnight bag that Sam had provided her. "What are we going to cook?" she asked as he escorted her outside.

The sky was nearly dark, but the half moon lit up the area. Almost all of the snow had melted, but with at least two more months of winter, more would be falling soon.

"What do you want to eat?" Sam asked as he held open the truck door. Of course, he wasn't looking at her, but rather he was scanning the area.

She touched his arm. "I don't sense any shifters, if that's who you're looking for."

He glanced down at her once she was seated. "I can't help it. It's who I am."

She could see that. Having someone always have her back was a comforting thought. "As for dinner, I'm up for anything."

The drive to the supermarket was a short one. With his arm around her waist, he led her inside. Given that Justin was out there somewhere, she'd been surprised Sam was willing to let her wander the aisles. He'd said since he was a military man he could handle a few punks in a public place. Since it was around dinnertime, she hadn't expected so many people. "I'll keep an eye out for Vinea," she said.

Sam looked down at her, pain in his eyes. "She has no need to harm you."

Lexi shrugged. "If she knows Justin, he might ask her to keep an eye on me."

Sam's hold tightened around her waist. "She better not, or she'll be sorry."

Lexi wanted to change the subject. This was supposed to be a romantic night. "So what are you in the mood for? And don't say you don't care."

"What can you cook?" he asked.

Lexi chuckled. She wasn't a great cook, but she wasn't bad either. "How about lasagna?"

"Works for me. Does that include garlic bread?" Sam didn't have an ounce of fat on him so maybe bread would be a treat.

"It's a given."

They headed to the pasta aisle for the noodles and sauce and then picked up the cheeses in the dairy section. The bread was next.

"I'll grab a bottle of red wine," he said.

As long as they were going all out, she wanted dessert. "Chocolate, berries, or apple pie?"

He chuckled. "They all sound good, but I do have a weakness for apple pie."

"Me too as long as there's some ice cream on top."

"Is there any other way to eat it?"

Sam was so easy to get along with. Once they collected the food, they checked out. While he had been subtle about it, as he passed each aisle, he glanced down each one, probably to make sure neither Vinea nor Justin were there.

Armed with two bags of groceries, they left. She couldn't wait to cook, eat, and then relax. Somewhere in there, she would temporarily satisfy her need for him, as her wolf was becoming more and more demanding.

Blue sparks shot off her hands at the thought of being with Sam forever, and a sly smile crossed his lips.

"What are you thinking about?" he asked with way too much cheer.

"My freedom. What else would I be thinking about?"

"With those sparks? I think you might have something else on your mind other than eating and freedom."

"I guess you'll just have to wait and see."

She swore his smile stayed put on his face for another mile, until he pulled into his garage. He grabbed both bags after handing her the keys to open up. The domestic move wasn't lost on her.

When they stepped inside she paid attention to whether there were any shifter signatures. Thankfully, she found nothing. "It's good."

"I want to do a quick sweep of the place anyway. I can't be too cautious where you are concerned."

Aw. He was the best. Once he placed the bags on the counter, she handed him back his keys. Sam checked each room, including those upstairs.

"All good?" she asked when he returned to the kitchen.

"Yes, but having confirmation that Kapok is in town has me on edge."

She wrapped her arms around his waist. "Can we forget him for a little while and just enjoy ourselves?"

Sam glanced down at her and smiled. "I'd like that."

As if they cooked together every night, they shrugged out of their coats then emptied the bags of groceries. "I'll put the ice cream in the freezer," he said.

She asked Sam to set the oven to 350° and to find a large pot for the noodles. Lexi explained how her mom used to make lasagna.

"You're in charge," he said. "My culinary skills don't extend much beyond breakfast,"

"I doubt that. You could do anything you set your mind to."

"Stay here long enough and you'll be testing that theory."

She was about to say that she wanted to, but it wasn't the right time for that conversation. Once the pasta was cooked, they worked together layering the noodles and spreading the cheeses and sauce. When the oven pre-heated, he placed the meal inside while she read the instructions for the garlic bread.

"I'll pour the wine," Sam said.

"Everything smells so good." After a few minutes, she tossed it into the oven with the lasagna.

"Your wine." Sam handed her a glass.

Lexi leaned against the kitchen counter and sipped her drink. The first taste went down so smoothly that she moaned. "Goddess, I needed this."

He ran a hand down her arm. "You've been a trooper through all this mess, but it should be over soon."

That was what he'd said a few days ago. "Crying or running away won't solve my problems. I still think drawing him out is the best thing—assuming we have backup ready to take him down."

"Like I said before, if we had a ton of members working for McKinnon and Associates, I might agree, but it could be days before Justin makes his move."

"I know, but it's frustrating."

He slipped her drink from her fingers and then set both glasses on the counter. Pulling her against his chest, she melted against him. "I thought you said you didn't want to discuss Justin," he said.

"I don't. He just keeps popping up at all the wrong times."

Sam smiled. "Then I guess I'll have to keep you occupied."

"Oh, yeah?" She'd like that.

He tapped her nose. "After we eat. Now what should we talk about?"

"If Justin is off limits, how about telling me about your time in the military?"

His eyes darkened, almost as if he was pulling down a shade, and his whole posture stiffened.

*Note to self: Don't ask about his time in the service.*

Sam forced his body to relax and looked at her with a gentle smile. "How about you tell me more about yourself?"

"You know everything about me."

"No I don't. What were you like as a kid—super popular, a jock, a nerd or what?"

Lexi finished off her glass of wine and Sam poured her another. "I was a little bit of everything I guess. When I would play with my friends, I always volunteered to be a teacher. Lynn liked to play shrink, and Lisa was the jock. I had a small chalkboard, and I'd have them do math problems for me—simple ones so they felt successful."

"That's so cute. You were a born teacher, and I was a born protector."

Funny how that worked. She searched for what else Sam might find interesting. "I played the piano from third grade to sixth grade until my teacher became ill. I didn't really have a knack for it anyway."

"Piano, huh? Mom made me play the guitar. I sucked at it too."

She was amazed at how much they had in common. "What foreign language did you study in school?"

"German. You?"

"French."

Sam smiled. "Here's the big question? What kind of movies do you like?" The oven timer buzzed. "Hold that thought. Food's ready. Then we talk." He retrieved the food and placed it on the two potholders on the table.

"I'll cut the bread." Working side by side reminded her of being with her mom when they would make fudge and chocolate chip cookies together on the weekends. Occasionally, her mother would let her help with the main meal, but that was only after Lexi turned about twelve.

"You're smiling," he said.

She placed the too hot bread on a plate. "Just thinking about my mom and how much she loved to cook."

"You're lucky. My mom wasn't very domestic. Dad actually was better at meal prep."

"Do you miss them?" Apparently, they'd been living in Florida for close to two years.

"I think I missed them more when I lived with them. As a kid, I wanted my parents to go to my soccer and baseball games. They did until I entered high school, but then stopped when they decided to turn their attention to teaching others."

The hurt in his voice pained her. "You and Teagan seemed to have turned out okay."

"I guess. It taught me to appreciate family, though I'm sure Teagan thought I had a funny way of showing it as I was overseas for much of the time."

"You're here now." Ronan always accused Lexi of looking at the bright side of things.

"True. Back to the question I asked," Sam said. "What kind of movies do you like?"

She chuckled. "Honestly? I'm into the animated 3-D ones and anything from Disney or Pixar."

"Me too!"

Most likely he was just saying that, but she appreciated it nonetheless. Knowing little things about him made him more human and less like this perfect specimen of a man.

They both dug into their meals. Lexi moaned at the divine combination of flavors. "I think this is the best lasagna I've ever made."

"It's fantastic. I should turn Italian so I have an excuse to have this every night."

Sam was so easy to please. Their talk turned to the men Sam worked with and how they had met their mates. She'd heard some of the stories from the women, but it was interesting to hear the male take on it.

"It seems to me that many of your male friends were in denial about even having a mate," she said.

"That's for sure. Kalan was the worst. As Beta of the Clan, he couldn't believe that he'd been paired with Elana—a human. Turns out it was the best thing that ever happened to him. Elana seems to really center him."

"How is he handling having a child and being a detective?" If she and Sam ended up together, she was curious how his job would impact their lives. Right now, he was never home since he was protecting her.

"It's hard, but they're figuring it out."

"When I went to the welcome party, only two of the women weren't mated."

He raised his brows. "Missy and who else?"

"Blair, Jackson's sister."

"Ah, yes, I forgot about her. She only moved to town recently. She and Ainsley, Jackson's mate, were roommates for years."

One more piece of the puzzle fell into place. "I was impressed with all the women. They seemed focused and highly competent."

"They are." He grabbed a piece of garlic bread and stuffed it in his mouth. Once he swallowed, he leaned back. "I haven't eaten like this in forever."

"It is good, isn't it?"

"Totally. You finished?" he asked, nodding to her plate.

"Yes."

Sam swallowed. "Me too."

Lexi pushed back her chair and together they placed the leftover food in the refrigerator and the dishes in the sink. She was about to rinse them and put them in the dishwasher when Sam touched her arm.

"Leave them. I can't wait any longer." A blue spark flitted off his arm.

"Wait any longer for what? To watch a movie?" She was pretty sure that wasn't what he meant, but she needed to hear him say that he was yearning for her as much as she was for him.

Sam's eyes shone bright. "For this."

He leaned over and kissed her, acting as if he needed the contact before being able to take another breath. The pressure against her chest caused her inner wolf to howl. With her back against the counter, she wrapped her arms around him and drew him even closer. Their tongues tangled, and the combination of red sauce, wine, and garlic made for a heady combination that caused lust and desire to swamp her with need.

Sam leaned back. "You don't know how hard it's been keeping away from you at work."

Really? She was the one who was the werewolf. She had to battle her pesky animal within her twenty-four hours a day, though it was possible her Wendayan side was adding to her need. That made sense if Sam was suffering too. The big question was did he know they were fated to be mates?

The answer to that didn't matter at the moment. What mattered was fucking him hard and fast to satisfy—however temporary—her intense urges. Lexi slipped her hands under his shirt and lifted it over his head in one quick movement. After dropping the shirt on the floor, she licked his nipple, and it instantly peaked.

"Hey, none of that. That's my job."

She grinned. "Really? I dare you to lick your own nipple."

"You're funny, sassy girl." Before she could reach the button on his jeans, he lifted her shirt over her head, and his eyes widened. A blue glow suddenly surrounded him. "Red? You know how to torment a guy, don't you?"

"I didn't know we'd be doing this when I dressed this morning."

"I guess I'm lucky."

"You are."

She finally made contact with his pants and managed to unbutton and unzip them, but she couldn't tug them off because Sam's hands were in the way, trying to take off her pants at the same time. In the end, they laughed too hard to be effective. He finally gave up and moved to higher ground.

When he lowered the bra straps down her shoulders, his touch nearly scorched her, and her wolf growled. Licking his lips, her libido shot sky high.

*Take him now*, her wolf pleaded.

Giving up trying to remove his heavy jeans, she reached into his briefs and grabbed his hot cock. She pumped her fist once, loving the sound of his grunt.

With Sam's eyes closed, both of their auras glowed blue. It was almost as if the goddess from above was adding lighter fluid to their fire.

"Kiss me again," she demanded as she let go of him.

Sam did, and his urgency thrilled her. He unhooked the front clasp and rubbed his thumbs across her distended nipples. Not able to last much longer, she kicked off her shoes, and then finished undoing the waistband of her jeans before tugging it low.

Sam stepped back. "Let me help."

When he dropped to his knees, her animal went wild. Her nails sharpened and her scalp itched—the precursor to shifting. In one slow drag, he took off both her pants and panties. She was so fucking ready for him that her arousal perfumed the air. "Please," she begged.

"Shh. Let me enjoy this moment."

He had no idea what it was like to have a mate so close and yet not be able to satisfy her immediate needs. Lexi inhaled and let his musky scent seep deep within her, swirling around her body until his very being was imprinted on her soul forever.

The first swipe of his tongue had her panting, and the second had her grabbing his hair and tugging hard. When her bones began to crack, she had to squeeze her eyes shut and force control back into her body.

He dipped two fingers into her while he flicked her nub back and forth with his tongue. Bending her knees slightly to change the angle only added to the glorious sensations coursing through her. It was when he pressed on that most sensitive spot that her release came hard and fast.

Her breath whooshed in and out as she tried to gain some control. "Now, Sam! Please!"

Sam stood, and without a word, ditched the rest of his clothes. "Come here."

He grabbed her close, and then lifted her up until her butt was touching the counter. On instinct, she wrapped her arms and legs around him.

Keeping his gaze on her face, he spun her around until her back was against the pantry door. "I hope you're ready."

"Bring it on, soldier."

# Chapter Sixteen

L EXI WAS IN heaven right now being in Sam's arms. With her
back pressed against the pantry door and her hands gripping his
shoulders, he dipped his head. The first tug on her nipple had her
spinning. Arching her back to give him easier access, Sam switched to
the other side and twisted the tip using his teeth, causing waves of
delight to spread over her. Desiring more, she wiggled her hips,
loving the pressure of his cock. But it wasn't enough. Needing some
control, Lexi pressed the soles of her feet onto his thighs and lifted
high enough to reach his cock.

"Lexi, be careful."

She'd be careful all right. She'd put it in a nice warm place.
Taking aim, she placed the tip of his cock at her entrance. Raising his
head, Sam drew her closer, and she slid down on him. Sparks flew.
Her pulse rose, and her wolf jumped for joy. Even before she lifted
up, she moaned as she ran her tongue against her sharpening teeth.

"Don't shift, Lexi. Not yet."

Her eyes must be pure amber or else he could hear her body
transforming. "I'm working hard not to, but it feels so fucking
good."

Sam plastered his lips to hers as he drove into her, taking her
higher with each stroke. It didn't matter she'd just climaxed. That
had merely shown her how much she needed him.

After he plowed into her again, she lifted and then dropped, all
the while devouring his kiss. He was the one to break the contact and

move his mouth to her neck. His lips suctioned the sensitive skin at the top of the collarbone before moving his mouth upward where he nibbled on the shell of her ear. Each lick and touch ignited her further. It was when he slammed his hips up against her, driving into her deeper than ever before, that she could no longer hold back. Her climax came in strong waves, transporting her to a place of love and freedom—a place she never wanted to leave.

Sam's hold tightened, and his near yell brought her back to the present as his hot cum pumped into her. When the flow stopped, she lowered her head onto his shoulder and waited for her breath to return to her body. Lexi wasn't even aware they'd moved positions until her butt hit the cold kitchen counter. From the drawer he retrieved a clean cloth, wet it, and cleaned them both up.

Finally, she was able to wrap her head around the amazing sex. Even her wolf was totally satisfied. "That was a great dessert," she said.

He grinned. "Indeed, but I still want my apple pie."

BOTH SAM AND Lexi propped their feet up on the coffee table enjoying their dessert. "I have to admit the vanilla ice cream adds a new dimension to the pie."

"I thought you always ate it that way," Lexi said.

"Nope, but when you mentioned it, I went along with it."

"I'm glad I was able to expand your horizons."

She'd expanded his horizons in many more ways than offering a different way to eat pie. He picked up the television remote. "What do you want to watch on television?"

"Are we spending the night here?"

"We could, I guess. I thought the longer we're here, the more normal your life will seem."

She smiled. "I appreciate it, but Justin is still out there. My life can't truly be normal until he's caught."

"Come here." He set down the remote and gathered her in his

arms. "Nothing is going to happen to you or me."

"Justin and his men are werewolves. They could tear you to pieces in a minute."

He stroked her face. "I can implant thoughts into their heads that tell them I'm not Sam Pompley, or that no one is standing in front of them. Hell, I can even read their minds a little bit." He told her what happened when Anna Fairchild had helped find something the Changelings wanted. When they came to take it away, he'd successfully convinced them that the sardonyx wasn't there.

"That's amazing. Okay, what am I thinking now?" she asked with total sincerity.

Maybe it was time to tell her the truth. Lexi was a wonderful woman who was brave and tough yet tender at the same time. "Hmm. You're thinking about my huge cock and how you'd like to make love with me again."

She burst out laughing. "That's not fair. I think I'm obsessed with your body. I can never get enough."

He grinned, in part because that might mean she realized they were mates too. "In all seriousness, there are some people I just can't read."

Her face lost some color. "What happens if you can't read Justin's mind?"

He blew out a breath. "He'll be no problem. My grandfather explained when I could and when I couldn't get into someone's head. While he didn't say this explicitly, I doubt I can put thoughts into the minds of gods or goddesses."

She laughed. "I can assure you I am not one of them, so no problem there."

"I figured. Naliana, the goddess who frequents Silver Lake on the white moon, has an immortal husband. While I've never tried to put thoughts into his head—because I've never met him—I doubt he'd be susceptible to my mind bending abilities either."

"But you can read everyone else, right?" She finished the last bit of her dessert and placed her plate next to his.

"Not quite. There's one other person that I can't affect." *Here goes.* "It's my mate."

Lexi stilled. He swore she stopped breathing until a giant smile spread across her face. "Are you saying you can't put thoughts into my head because I am your mate?"

Sam returned her grin. "Seems so."

Her shoulders sagged. "Is that the only way you can tell?"

"Relax." He stroked her arm. "If you're wondering if I'm like a shifter who becomes *obsessed*—your word—with finding then being with his mate, then yes." He held up hand. "There are differences between my kind and a shifter though. While I love how your skin tastes and smells, I didn't notice that you were my mate when I first met you because of your scent, like most shifters do."

She cracked up. "I should hope not. I was layered in garbage."

"I meant after that, silly. Bottom line, I know you're my mate by more than one factor. It's not only because I can't warp your mind."

"Why didn't you tell me earlier? It would have saved me a lot of wondering."

Now it was his turn to stop breathing. "Are you saying you know I'm your mate?"

"Yes. If I didn't, I never would have trusted you like I do. The moment we met, I knew there was something different about you. Mind you, I was a bit preoccupied after crawling out of the trash bin."

Lexi was something else. "I can only imagine. Being sold and then having someone rob you gives you every right to be preoccupied."

"Why did you wait so long to tell me?" She straddled him and his body shot to life again.

He clasped her waist because it was the safest place for his hands. "Did you forget that you had other things to worry about? Like a crazy man who was out to kidnap and whisk you back to Vermont?"

"Hardly, but if you'd told me, it would have been one less thing to worry about."

"I'm sorry. At the time, I figured the last thing either of us needed was to become so blinded by lust that we became distracted." He cupped her face. "Once this mess with Justin Kapok is finished, we can talk about mating and what we want to do with the rest of our lives." Sam watched Lexi as she turned and looked away. "What? You don't want to mate with me?"

Maybe that was why she hadn't.

"No! Of course, I want to mate with you. I agree we should wait till this whole Justin thing is settled though. Plus, when I left my home, I was headed to Florida. Since I was little, I have always wanted to live there. I still would like to visit, since I will be making a life here with you."

If she felt that strongly about it, then now might be a good time to fly down there for a few days. They'd have a fun vacation and visit his parents. Since returning from his service in the war, he hadn't taken much time to enjoy himself either. "How would you like it if we took a three or four day vacation to Florida?"

Her eyes shone brightly. "Really?" she asked.

"Yes. I'd consider moving there for good if I had could get work there, but I'll admit that I love Silver Lake. I have the best job in the world. Not only is Teagan here, this is my home."

Lexi hugged him. "You are amazing. I can't wait to go. When can we leave?"

"I'll check flights tomorrow."

She ran a hand down his chest. "When we get back, will you teach me to shoot?"

"What? Where did that come from?"

She lifted a shoulder. "You know I want to. With so much danger swirling around, I thought I should know how to protect myself."

"I'll think about it." He wasn't sure it was a good idea, though why he couldn't say. "You'll have to get your concealed weapons' permit if you expect to carry."

"Hmm. Will you help me?"

He smiled. "Of course I will."

She kissed him. "Then I want to do it."

"Okay then. Silver Lake has both an indoor and an outdoor range."

"Perfect. You won't be upset if I end up a better shot than you, will you?"

Sam laughed. He did love his woman. "That will never happen."

She tapped his chest. "Don't be so sure, Sam Pompley."

NO MATTER HOW disgusted Vinea was at the actions of those two lovers, she couldn't help but listen to their conversation through the device Devon had provided her. If he ever learned that the equipment had been for Sam instead of Justin, Devon would come after her. Hell, he'd probably try to kill her. Poor soul would be so disappointed when he failed.

The sounds of sex finally stopped and Vinea let out a breath.

She could hear her sister now. "You're just jealous because they're enjoying themselves, and you'll always be alone."

That was crap. Vinea had no use for a man. Her jealousy of her sister existed because Vinea was ambitious. There was nothing wrong having that trait. In her opinion, wanting something and not working for it deserved to be called jealousy. That wasn't Vinea's problem. She worked her ass off only to have the prize given to someone else—namely her younger sister. Vinea vowed she'd be the best. Too bad Naliana and she had different definitions of what that meant.

Lexi squealed at something Sam said, and Vinea returned her focus to them. Not only had she planted the devices on each of the windows at Sam's house, she'd bugged his truck when it was parked in front of the office. The conversation he and Lexi had on the way to his house hadn't been the least bit interesting. She didn't give a flying fuck what they liked to eat or what kind of movies they enjoyed.

What did catch her interest was what they had just said—that they planned to be away for a few days. This would give her and Justin time to create a foolproof plan. Her mind had spun the moment Sam mentioned he'd take Lexi shooting. Vinea would question some locals to find out the best place to shoot. Seeing how much the people around here liked to hunt, the town probably had a designated area where one could practice. Assuming he took her outdoors, away from everyone, Vinea would strike.

Her heart pumped hard at her near victory. Yes! It was time to make sure Justin and his men would be ready. Vinea didn't want to be stuck in this hellhole any longer than necessary. She had other important work to do.

Vinea smiled. When Naliana learned what she'd done, Vinea's retribution would be complete. She couldn't wait.

# Chapter Seventeen

LEXI WAS SO excited. Not only would Justin go crazy trying to figure out where she'd disappeared to, she and Sam would have the most romantic and wonderful vacation in sunny Florida with no worries, lots of romantic walks on the beach, and tons of hot sex.

Sam even promised they'd go shopping for a bathing suit and some summer clothes once they arrived. According to the weather report, the temperatures were supposed to be in the mid seventies in Daytona Beach. To her that was perfect. While she felt a little bad leaving Connor, Kip, and Devon to answer the phone, Connor assured her the three of them could handle it. After all, they had done it before she took the job.

After a layover in Atlanta, the plane landed smoothly in Daytona Beach. As soon as they exited the airport, the warm, humid air sent shivers of delight straight through her. "It's wonderful."

"I will admit, a thirty degree change in temperature is nice, but don't get too used to it." He winked.

While she would take advantage of the warmth and absorb all that a Florida beach town had to offer, the best part was that she and Sam were here together. Lexi had to admit that Silver Lake had grown on her, though if she could move about freely, she might really enjoy more of what the town had to offer.

Sam had rented a car even though his folks said they could pick them up. "When did you last see your parents?" she asked.

"A few months ago. They had a break in their schedule and

drove up to see me and Teagan."

"How did that go?"

Sam smiled. "It was actually great. They really seemed focused on what my plans were and not on trying to convince me that I needed to do a past life regression in order to see where all my stress was coming from."

As much as Lexi tried to embrace what all witches did, she didn't understand a lot of it. "I've done a past life regression, and I have to admit it was quite enlightening."

"I'm glad."

Sam pulled into the mall parking lot. Lexi had only filled half her suitcase knowing she'd need to buy some summer clothes. While she didn't have a ton of money, it was enough for a few pairs of shorts, a bathing suit, and some lightweight tops.

He cut the engine. "Ready?"

"Yes, but don't worry about having to wait while I try on everything. I'm a quick shopper." She chuckled. "I don't like to shop."

"Well, I do."

They both laughed. These four days would be ones she would remember for a long time.

"SO, LEXI, TELL me how you met my son," Mrs. Pompley asked.

Sam huffed out a breath. When he'd called his folks to let them know he and Lexi would be visiting, he'd said she had a stalker and that they wanted to lay low for a few days. This wasn't supposed to be meet-my-mate time. Hell, he didn't even mention the word *mate* to his mother. She better not embarrass him by asking what his intentions were toward Lexi.

Lexi glanced over at him, and he nodded. One thing about his parents, they were good at keeping secrets.

"I was dumpster diving, and Sam came to my rescue." She held up a hand. "In my defense, I was in my wolf form."

The looks on his parents' faces were priceless, and he needed to explain. "What she meant was that her car broke down in the alley behind McKinnon's Pub and Pool, and she was trying to find something to eat. When I found out why she was on the run, I offered to let her stay at the McKinnon and Associates' safe house."

His mom reached out and clasped his hand. "You're a good man, son."

"Thank you."

His mother faced Lexi. "So have you contacted your mother about meeting your mate?"

Sam nearly spit out his drink. "Mom. How do you—?"

She smiled then looked over at his dad. "Why it's as clear as the nose on your face."

Whether that was true or not, now wasn't the time to discuss it—or ever. Talking about his lust and need wasn't a topic he was comfortable with. "Fine, we are mates, but we haven't mated. Lexi is trying to deal with this man who wants her for his own but don't worry. I won't let that happen."

"I'm glad. So Lexi, if you want to speak with your mother about—"

Lexi shook her head. "My mother passed away a few years ago."

"I know. I can sense that her spirit is around you though. Just because you can't pick up a phone and call her doesn't mean you can't speak with her."

Sam was used to his parents being *out there*, but he didn't want to scare Lexi away. Even though she was a witch, her talents extended to the physical and not the metaphysical.

Lexi clasped her glass with both hands. "What do you mean I can contact her?"

"Once we have dessert, I'll explain. We can try to contact her then."

She smiled. "I'd like that very much. Thank you."

"Evan, why don't you get the dessert, and I'll clear the table?" his mom asked.

Sam jumped up. "I'll help."

Lexi stood. "Me too."

When his mom grinned, all doubts about bringing Lexi to meet his parents disappeared. Together they cleared the table and put the dishes in the dishwasher while his dad pulled the pie out of the refrigerator.

"Your mom made your favorite dessert," his dad said.

"That would be apple pie," Lexi chimed in smiling.

"I see you know Sam well." His parents laughed together.

Once they finished cleaning up dinner and then ate a fabulous dessert—albeit without the ice cream topping—they headed to the living room. His mother located a candle along with a crystal on a string then motioned for them to sit across from her on the sofa.

After lighting the candle, his mom said some incantation words and then held up the crystal. "Lexi, ask your mother a question that can be answered with a yes or no response. If the crystal swings toward you, it represents a yes."

Even though Sam knew his mom could reach the spiritual world, he had never actually witnessed her contacting anyone before. He watched Lexi, hoping this experience wouldn't be too painful for her. His mother should have warned him that she planned to do this.

"Are you feeling any pain, Mom?" Lexi asked.

He'd never asked how her mother had died, but given her young age, he figured it was an accident or something like cancer.

The crystal slowly moved and the pendulum swung toward his mother.

"She says no, though if she is in a good place, she wouldn't feel any pain."

"I wish I could just ask her questions," Lexi said. "Yes or no is so limiting."

His mom stilled. "She's here."

Lexi grabbed Sam's hand. "What do you mean she's here?"

"Her essence is in the room. I can feel her. She's telling me that she's surprised you aren't pummeling her with questions that have a yes or no answer because you think so logically."

"I'm a bit overwhelmed," Lexi said, her voice sounding a bit shaky.

"I understand," his mom said then looked upward. "Your mother says she's sorry about your dad. She had no idea he'd return to his old habits after she died."

Lexi's grip tightened. "So Bill drank and gambled a lot before you died? I knew he had a cocktail or two when he came home from work, but that was all." Sam's mom nodded. "Do you think I should go back home and help him?"

Sam held his breath. Lexi's face paled. She didn't need to be going through this after all she'd been through.

"She says you need to seek out your own happiness," his mother said. Her shoulders slumped, and the pace of her breathing picked up. She then returned her focus to Lexi. "She's gone."

Lexi released her grip. "I felt her too. Thank you."

His mother blew out the candle. "Your mother was very serene, more so than most. She did say one last thing, and that was not to lose touch with your brother."

"I won't." Thankfully Lexi smiled, even though it was fleeting.

His mom was amazing, and he would have to thank her for helping Lexi make contact.

# Chapter Eighteen

LEXI LOVED FLORIDA, but she realized two things as she and Sam walked hand in hand along the shore. Being with someone as special as Sam made the experience that much more rewarding and romantic. Secondly, her skin wasn't made to be in the sun for so many hours. While she didn't mind the humidity, her hair hated it. She might have to be content to just visit Florida during the winter, but live in Tennessee the rest of the year—assuming Justin was caught.

Sam tugged on her hand. "The waves are picking up. Let's go in again."

While the water wasn't as warm as she'd hoped, compared to the icy coast of Vermont, this was tepid. Together they plowed through the water, stopping and turning to the side when the wave swelled. Once they were past the two-foot waves, she bent her knees until the water was up to her neck.

"Come here, you." Sam grabbed her, clasped her to his chest, and kissed her. Seagulls squawked overhead, and kids squealed less than twenty feet away.

"Mmm," she moaned. Right now, it was as if the world had ceased to exist except for the two of them.

When the waves separated them, he smiled. "Are you having a good time?"

She moved closer and then wrapped her arms and legs around him, hoping no one could tell what was going through her mind right about then. "Totally. This trip has been wonderful in every sense of the word. Not only did I find your parents charming, this beach is spectacular, and the company is amazing."

He grinned. "It was good for both of us. I don't think I'm ready to go back to Tennessee."

She furrowed her brows. "What are you saying? You want to move here?"

"I'd love to, but I can't. If I lived here, I'm afraid I'd never be able to stay focused on my work. I'd want to enjoy the beach every day."

"I feel the same way. If I had a teaching job, I'd be dreaming about walking on the warm sand and playing in the water."

His hands roamed down to her waist, and when he cupped her butt and drew her closer, his now-evident erection caused her wolf to go wild. "Do you know what I'd like to do now?" he asked.

Happiness soared through her. "Do I get three guesses?"

Sam walked them toward shore. "I don't think you need that many."

Releasing her when a wave crested, they rode the waves back to shore. When they reached their towels, they dried off and headed to their hotel, located just steps from the beach.

While the room had been expensive, Sam said it might be a long time before they returned. She'd agreed since her new mantra was all about embracing the moment.

Lexi would have suggested they shower first, but she couldn't wait to make love with Sam. He was too enticing, alluring, and so fucking sexy that if she didn't have him right now, she'd be in her wolf form in a heartbeat. What consequences that would have, she didn't know, but she didn't want to find out.

"Your trunks are still wet," she announced a second before she tugged them down. His cock was at attention and sparks were shooting off everywhere.

He laughed. "We need to shower first. I think I have sand in every crack and crevice of my body."

She did too. Lexi plastered her chest to his and wrapped her arms around his neck. "I don't want to be away from you for that long."

He untied the straps around her neck and lowered them. Without undoing the clasp in back, he stepped away from her then leaned over and licked one cold nipple. "Mmm, salty."

His slightly pinched brow implied it wasn't even close to being enjoyable. She chuckled. "Fine, we'll shower."

"I want to make love to you this instant, but trust me, you won't be happy if I don't clean up first."

She loved how he wanted to pass the blame onto himself. Hand in hand, he led her to the shower tub where he turned on the water. While it warmed, he finished stripping her in a slow, sensual manner. "Good choice on the bathing suit. It shows off your perfect body," he said as he raked his gaze over her from head to toe.

She was anything but perfect, but if Sam liked her shape, that was all that mattered. "I'm glad you like it."

Once Sam lowered her bottoms, she stepped out of them. He then yanked back the shower curtain and motioned she step in first.

Once under the warm spray, Lexi's muscles relaxed. Until now, she hadn't realized she'd been so chilled. She moaned and ran her hands over her body to get rid of the sand. Lexi could stay there for hours, but she didn't want to take too long. Sam was waiting.

He was watching her with pure lust in his eyes, "Feel good?" he asked as he switched places with her and washed.

"Yes, but I can think of a better place to put my hands though." She grabbed his cock and dropped to her knees. "I think you missed a spot."

Before he could stop her, she swiped her tongue from his balls to the tip. His groan was her reward.

Sam clutched a handful of her hair and tugged. She swirled her tongue around his cock as she pumped her fist up and down.

"I'm not going to last," he groaned out. A second later, his cock blew, spewing his hot seed up and over her hand.

Lexi smiled. "I guess you weren't kidding."

He pulled her to her feet. "Hurry up and finish washing woman, you got some hard loving coming your way." He grinned, poured a palm full of liquid soap, and cleaned his cock.

After she ducked under the water, she lathered her hair, while Sam finished washing. Then they switched places so she could rinse her hair. While she was under the water, he ran his soapy hands down her back, waking up her contented animal.

"Someone's excited," Sam said.

Only then did Lexi notice all the sparks shooting off her. Her nails and teeth were transforming too. "I am."

While she scrubbed her face and front, Sam washed what was facing him. The problem came when he dragged the soap between her legs, and her wolf inwardly howled.

She stepped around behind him and went to work on his back and sandy legs. Between the two of them, they finished in less than five minutes. By the time he turned off the water, her body was vibrating, and their need for each other was almost unbearable. As they dried each other, the sexual electricity sparking between them was pulsing in waves of blue.

Sam cupped her shoulders, pressed her against the vanity, and when he kissed her, Lexi's heart and soul spun with joy and elation. Needing more of him, she ran her hands up and down the planes of his corded back. Sam was everything she wanted in a man and in a mate, but before she mated with him, she needed to hear him say that he loved her.

Reaching between them, she grabbed Sam's cock again.

"None of that. This time, we do it my way." He stepped back, and then lifted her in his arms.

Once he placed her on the bed, Sam's lustful gaze traveled down her body once more. "I'm going to make a meal out of you."

His mere words heated her up further. Lexi spread her legs in an open invitation and gave him a sassy grin. "Welcome to your very own buffet; help yourself."

"Oh, baby, that is music to my ears." Sam pounced and spread her legs wider.

Anticipation soared, and the first swipe did not disappoint. Lexi bucked her hips upward and dug her fingers into his skin. Her scalp itched. On the next few licks, her glow continued to expand. Not wanting to hurt him with her newly sharp nails, she clutched the spread again. It almost wasn't fair that Sam already had a release. It meant he'd be able to last longer.

"I'm ready," she panted.

Sam reached up and kneaded her right breast as he continued the sensual assault on her clit. Waves of lust swamped her, and she had to work hard not to come. *You don't have to hold back*, her wolf said.

With his free hand, Sam slipped a finger inside her, and her orgasm immediately came crashing down. Lexi opened her mouth to draw in more air as she arched her back, pressing hard against his mouth and finger.

Sam somehow knew when to stop to prevent her wolf from having her way. With his gaze on her, Sam crawled on top, and his thick shaft slid right into her wetness. Holy hell. "That feels so good," she whispered.

Sam's lips met hers and together they embarked on an erotic journey, kissing and thrusting. With each plunge she soared higher and higher. His glow grew too until both of their orbs touched and then combined.

*Mate, mate*, her wolf urged. *Bite him.*

*Not yet*, she cautioned.

Sam lifted his head and groaned. When he closed his lids, the lines around his eyes disappeared. "Yeah, baby. That's it."

Lexi pressed her heels into the mattress and lifted up once more. She met his thrust with one of her own, causing them to explode at the same time. His hot seed streamed inside her, and her orgasm took control and sent her soaring.

Holding her tight, Sam rolled them over so that she was on top. "I love you, Lexi Laramie. I know you might think it's too soon, that there is no such thing as love at first sight, but I can't help how I feel."

While she could tell he really cared for her, never did she expect him to tell her that he loved her so soon. "I hope when you first saw me in that dumpster, you weren't enamored."

"It happened after you showered." He grinned.

She chuckled. "As long as we're confessing, I love you too."

"You really do?"

He didn't have to act so surprised. "Yes. I thought I'd shown you in many ways."

Sam grinned and joy spread across his face. "You have, but I don't want you to say it just because I said it first."

Men never cared about those kinds of things. "That's just silly."

"I'll show you silly, but first I need a towel."

He pulled out and dashed to the bathroom. Once they cleaned up, Sam sat on the bed opposite her. "Are you hungry?"

"You should know by now that I'm always up for food, especially after having amazing sex."

"Then come on. We'll see what restaurants are nearby."

# Chapter Nineteen

RETURNING TO SILVER Lake was bittersweet. Sam had enjoyed visiting with his parents who for the first time seemed excited about returning to Tennessee when their teaching term ended. They said that seeing Sam with Lexi made them realize that they wanted their family to be together, and that when their grandchildren arrived, they didn't want to miss out. Sam assumed they were thinking about Teagan and Kip, though if Lexi were willing, he'd love to have a few little soldiers to train.

No sooner had their plane touched down in Knoxville than the lines around her eyes and mouth tightened. Even as they walked through the terminal, Lexi stayed vigilant, clearly expecting Justin to materialize at any moment.

Sam wrapped his free arm around her shoulders. "I doubt Justin will try anything in this sea full of people."

"Probably not, but just knowing we're back has me on edge."

He wished he could turn around and fly back to Florida, but they couldn't hide forever. They exited the airport, and he located his parked truck quickly. After he paid his fee at the tollbooth, he headed back home, making sure to check for anyone suspicious in his rear view mirror.

Much of the last snowfall had melted, but the weather forecast claimed they were in for another storm to hit this weekend. Being office bound would really bum Lexi out, but it couldn't be helped. "If the weather cooperates, how about I show you how to shoot a gun tomorrow?"

Her face instantly brightened. "Really? I'd love that."

As Silver Lake came into view, all looked calm. No red or white moon in the sky to cause the Changelings or the crazies to be about. "I think we should spend the night in the safe room. Are you okay with that?" He doubted she'd argue. Lexi understood the risks.

"I'm good either way. I've had my taste of freedom, and it was wonderful, but I know Justin will be chomping at the bit to try something. Unless he has found a group of people to swindle out of their money, he's losing a lot being in Silver Lake."

"We haven't come across any gambling syndicates, but it's possible they exist. If he's in a nearby town, he has more freedom to ask around."

Sam pulled into the lot, but this time he decided to park in the garage.

"Is there a reason why we're hiding?" she asked, an edge creeping into her voice.

He reached out and rubbed her leg. "Just being precautious." If they were going to be in the open tomorrow, it would be best if Justin didn't know they'd arrived back in town—assuming he was keeping track of their whereabouts. Kapok was a gambler, not a sophisticated investigator, or so he believed.

After an amazingly sound sleep, Lexi awoke a bit disoriented and alone. Heart pounding, she bolted upright. "Sam?"

Only after she received no answer did it register in her addled brain that she was at the safe house. Letting out a big breath, she checked the clock on the nightstand. It read a little past ten in the morning. No wonder Mr. Military man wasn't still in bed. He was probably upstairs taking care of business.

Feeling safe, Lexi stretched, yawned, and then crawled out of bed. When she opened her suitcase, she sighed just looking at the shorts and summer tops. More vacations to the beach were in her future, but for now, Silver Lake would be her home.

Today, Sam would be teaching her how to shoot outdoors, which meant she needed to wear her warmest clothes. After she washed up and dressed, she headed upstairs carrying her coat. Sam was standing in front of the coffee machine.

He spun around and smiled. "I thought I'd have to wake you. Sleep well?"

"Too well. I must have been more exhausted than I thought."

"I'm not surprised. Travel is always hard on the body. Do you want a cup of coffee before we head out?"

"Yes, please."

He poured her a cup. "How about if we grab a bite to eat at the café, and then head out for your shooting lesson?"

"Sounds perfect. I trust you have a gun for me to use?"

He brought the two coffees over to the table. "I have several for you to choose from."

Lexi sat across from him and marveled how far she'd come in such a short period. In the past, trusting a man wasn't in her DNA, but Sam had taught her to trust her instincts. Perhaps it was because he was a Wendayan that she believed he'd always be there for her. Once the coffee cooled enough to drink, she guzzled it down, the flavor different from the usual kind here. "I like this. What is it?"

"Hazelnut. Kip brought it in."

"Nice."

"Ready?" he asked after he rinsed out both of their mugs and then set them on a paper towel to dry.

"Yes."

They left through the back of the building in order to reach the underground garage. Her car sat in one bay, Sam's truck in another one, but the last two spaces were empty. She vaguely remembered him saying that they were reserved for Connor's and Jackson's dads when they were in town. Parking in a garage was much nicer than having to scope out the parking lot in front every time they left. Once he pulled out, sunlight streamed into the truck.

"Are you excited?" he asked.

"About learning to shoot?" He nodded. "I think I'm more excited just to be outside with you."

He flashed her a smile. They headed east toward the restaurant. Because it was in the middle of the week, there were a lot of parking places in front when they arrived. Sam pulled into a free space.

As soon as she stepped outside, she sensed someone. A moment later, an older man rounded the corner, and when Sam waved, she relaxed. "Do you know him?"

"Yes, he's a friend of Connor's dad." Sam held open the café door and motioned she enter first.

Inside, she detected a few shifter signatures, but clearly these folks hadn't followed them here.

The café smelled of coffee and eggs, and her stomach responded with a grumble. She was so ready to eat. The sign at the front said to seat themselves, so Sam led her toward the back.

As soon as they sat, their server rushed over with a pot of coffee. "I'll be back in a jiffy to take your order," she said.

Should Justin try to take her against her will, Lexi wanted to understand Sam's capabilities better. "What would you do if Justin and his men walked into this café and demand I go with them?"

"Would you go with them?"

Anger rushed to the surface. "No! Of course not, but since I can't exactly shift in front of the townsfolk, he could drag me away—until you could stop them. I'm strong, but I can't take down several men."

Sam picked up his cup and blew on the steam billowing off the top. "For starters, the folks of Silver Lake would never let that happen, but yes I would do my mind bending on them."

She looked around. All of the male customers were in their sixties. "He might have a gun."

"That wouldn't make a difference. I would infiltrate his mind, and the mind of the others, and convince them that a pile of vipers was on your seat instead of you."

"Eww."

"Don't take it personally. From experience, I find people want to get the hell away from slithering reptiles. Just in case Kapok and his men don't get the hint to keep their distance, I'd add an additional thought that Justin no longer wants you."

"That would be sweet." Thank goodness Sam couldn't read or alter her mind. She'd never know what was true and what wasn't.

"So you see, you have nothing to worry about."

She leaned back in her seat. More relaxed than she had been, she picked up her menu and scanned the offerings. Everything looked fantastic. When the server returned, Lexi had to pick a dish. "I'll have the spinach and feta cheese omelet with the avocado slices on top. For my side, how about a cup of fresh fruit and an English muffin."

"Perfect. And for you, Sam?"

Did all the women know him?

"Let me have the cinnamon pancakes with a side of sausage."

The waitress nodded and left. "How do you eat so much and stay fit?" she asked.

"I'm usually more disciplined, but I treat myself every once in a while."

"I try to eat healthy most of the time." Okay, maybe the English muffin wasn't, but the rest was good for her. Lexi leaned forward on her elbows. "On a different note, has Connor said anything to you about spending so much time with me? I mean you do have to work for your salary."

"Relax. It's all good. Connor understands what we're up against. He'd never leave anyone in need stranded."

"He seems like a good man."

"I would have been proud to serve with him."

What a great sentiment. "Okay, but after today, you need to get back to work. I'm good with hiding out for a while."

He laughed. "If you say so."

Their meals arrived shortly and they both inhaled their food. In no time, the omelet and the pancakes were history. Lexi polished off her cup of coffee, ready for her next adventure.

Sam waved for the check, but this time she dug her hand in her purse. "I want to pay."

"Not going to happen."

"But you shouldn't have to pay all the time."

He reached out and cupped her hand. "How about if I want to treat? Look, if you want to make it fair, you can cook me a meal at home."

She guessed that was an equitable exchange. "Okay, and thank you."

This time when they stepped outside, Lexi also searched the streets, but her senses didn't detect any shifters.

"Looks clear," Sam said as he escorted her to the truck.

After driving south through town, the well-traveled roads soon turned to dirt, and she focused on the stunning landscape of rolling hills and tall pines. "Where are we headed?"

"A place next to where the caves are located. There's a good place to practice in peace."

"Sounds awesome."

Less than ten minutes later the well-packed dirt road turned more pitted, but with all the snow packed between the rocks, it wasn't a terribly bumpy ride. When they reached the end, Sam cut the engine. "This is as far as we go. We're hoofing it from here."

From the back, Sam retrieved a duffel bag and slung it over his shoulder.

"That bag looks full. How many guns did you bring?" she asked.

"Only four. There are three for you to pick from, and then one for me to use. Most of the space is taken up with the metal targets."

He was really serious about teaching her. Together, they hiked up the path that was surrounded by conifers. The pine scented the air, and other than a few small animals darting in the woods, it was eerily quiet. "It's so peaceful here."

Sam smiled. "It's one of my favorite spots in Silver Lake."

For the next twenty minutes, they trudged up the path covered with patches of snow. By the time they reached the large, flat field, Lexi was actually warm. Sam set down the bag and extracted three guns.

"These aren't loaded. I want you to pick them up and tell me if one feels better to you. The weight distribution will be different for different people."

Excited, Lexi lifted each one and took aim before deciding. "I like this one the best."

"Good, I figured you would. Let me show you how to load the magazine." Not surprising, Sam turned out to be a patient teacher. "Before I show you the proper way to shoot, I need to put up the targets. Do you want to help?"

"Absolutely."

It seemed no matter what they did—talking over coffee, walking along the beach, or hiking in the snow—they always had fun. Just being with Sam gave her such joy.

Once he reached some mystical spot, he opened his bag and snapped a metal circle onto a post. "Walk about twenty feet and jam this into the ground."

Even though the dirt was mostly frozen, a few taps with a large rock was enough to drive the stake into the ground. She silently thanked her ancestors for having magical strength. Once she was finished, he motioned her to return to their original spot.

"For your first lesson, face the target squarely and spread your feet apart about shoulder width." He demonstrated, and she tried to mimic what he was doing. "Next, grip the gun with your dominant hand and then, holding your arms out straight, wrap your hand around the other one for support." She attempted to do as he said, but apparently her form wasn't up to par, because Sam had to show her.

He stood behind and reached around her. He then adjusted her grip and finger position. While she was tempted to wiggle her butt, she refrained. He was doing her a favor by bringing her here and teaching her.

"So I'm ready to shoot?" she asked.

"Not yet. Line up the sight with your target."

"Didn't you say you had ear protection for us?" she asked.

"Oh, shit. I wasn't thinking. Yes." He located the earmuffs and placed one pair over her head and one on his. "Give it a try."

Suddenly, Lexi was a bit nervous. Looking down the sight, she inhaled then pulled the trigger. The kickback was stronger than she'd expected, but she only took one step back. "Do you think I hit the target?" she asked.

"I don't think so. Let me show you how you can tell."

Sam withdrew his weapon, and in one smooth motion lifted his arms, took aim, and fired three shots in rapid succession. The loud blasts were followed by three high-pitched pings.

Duh. The bullets would make a sound. "You're really good."

"Don't worry. With practice, you can be too."

Did he think she planned on practicing for a few years? She might if she enjoyed it. For the next half hour, Lexi worked on improving, but only hit the target three times. "My arms are tired. Plus, I need to take a pee break."

Sam swung his arm around. "Take your pick; there are plenty of trees."

Mostly trees with no leaves, though the chances of someone else happening upon her when her pants were down were slim, but she wanted to find a secure place for her peace of mind. She pointed to some undergrowth that might make a good shield. "I'll wander over there."

"I'll pack up."

Lexi headed to the tree line. When her first location seemed to require some tricky footing to step close to the bush, she moved farther away to a large oak tree with a thick trunk. This was perfect. Once she finished doing her business, she zipped up. Before she could step from behind the tree, low growls sounded and a human shouted. Then Sam emitted a painful wail, and her heart nearly stopped.

# Chapter Twenty

A T THE COMBINATION of violent sounds, Lexi froze, her mind spinning with sheer horror. Those were Sam's cries. Pulse soaring, she rushed back through the woods. Through the leafless forest, she could see bits and pieces of the fight as Sam battled the wolves. Her heart was in her stomach as fear for his survival nearly strangled her.

When she reached the scene, Sam had managed to toss off one wolf and was struggling with another. Two other wolves entered from the side, possibly waiting for their turn to attack. Just as she was about to shift into her wolf form and do what she could, Justin stepped out from behind a tree.

"That's enough," he commanded.

The one wolf that Sam had tossed to the ground slithered away on his stomach as if he were stunned. The second wolf clinging to Sam's back jumped off. A second later, Sam's knees hit the ground, and then he collapsed onto his back.

Lexi wanted to rush to him, but her leg muscles froze, and her hands both shook so hard, she couldn't think straight. Blood was smeared over his face and jacket, and his eyes remained closed. Why hadn't he tried to control their minds?

She spun around to face Justin. "Why did you hurt him?"

"You're a hard woman to get close to. You have no idea the problems I've had to deal with in order to retrieve you."

Tough shit. He moved closer, and she held up her palms. "Stay where you are."

Justin actually halted. "What are you going to do? Fight me, little girl?"

He had no idea what she was capable of. She glanced over at Sam. His head was turned to the side, but his eyes were now open. He was looking at the wolves that were keeping guard over him. They growled and then backed away. One yelped as if in pain. Without looking at Justin, they turned and trotted off.

"Hey, where the hell are you going?" Justin's hands clenched at the betrayal.

She puffed out her chest, trying to act as if she'd caused the wolves to go off. "I scared them off. They won't be coming back either."

The third and fourth wolves slowly followed suit. Justin called after them, but it was as if they'd gone deaf.

Justin returned his attention to her. "I don't fucking care what you did. Hell, it makes you more desirable."

Damn. She debated telling him Sam had used his mind control on the wolves, but she feared Justin would figure out a way to exploit him. She just wished Sam had used his talent sooner.

"You're coming with me, or I'll finish off both you and your so-called boyfriend, who by the way doesn't look too hot right now."

She looked back over her shoulder. Sam groaned, and his eyes fluttered closed once more, as blood continued to stain the ground around him. As much as she wanted to go to him, she had to keep Justin at bay. Getting ready to shift, she slipped off her jacket and tried not to wince when the cold air bit into her skin.

"Even if I came with you, what do you hope to accomplish?" she asked. "Sam and I are already mated." Unless he checked Sam for her wolf marking on his shoulder, he'd never know that was a lie.

Justin laughed. "Nice try, but no you aren't."

"How do you know? We just returned from our honeymoon in Florida." She gave him her gotcha look, but his expression didn't change.

"Again, no."

"How do you know?" Stomach acid burned in her gut, and she worked hard to keep from shifting. She wanted answers.

"We bugged Sam's truck."

Her heart nearly stopped at those words. "I don't believe you."

"So now the liar is calling me a liar?" He scratched his chin as if stalling for time. "I can prove it. You talked about the time you and Ronan made this big elaborate plan to run away, but in the end you chickened out."

Oh, shit, she had told that story to Sam about her childhood. "So, that's how you knew where we'd be today," she said more to herself than to him.

Anger at the invasion stabbed her. For that transgression and many others, Justin would have to die. In a flash, she was in her wolf form. Lexi charged. Right before she reached him, he shifted too. Because Justin managed to change right before they collided, her full frontal assault missed. She spun back around to try again. Teeth gnashed, and as he swiped a paw at her, she ducked and dodged trying to become as unavailable as possible. Instead of retreating and coming at him again, she swiped her paw across his eyes, and his yelp gave her a boost. While he'd heal quickly, his temporarily clouded vision would help her take him down.

Reveling in her success instead of planning her next attack, Justin lunged, getting the drop on her. When he clamped down on her neck, the pain nearly paralyzed her. If she didn't get out of his hold soon, she'd die.

Focusing on saving Sam, adrenaline flooded her system. She swiped at Justin's front legs, and her claws lodged into his flesh. He opened his mouth for a split second and yelped. Disengaging from his painful bite, she danced out of reach but then staggered. That bite on her neck must have done more damage than she realized. Her strength was draining fast. It didn't matter that she was imbued with more strength than the average wolf; a well-aimed bite could kill her. She had to finish him off soon or he'd kill Sam.

Picturing the man she loved as they walked along the beach, she would use all of her remaining energy to take down this bastard or die trying. Lexi lunged, and pain sliced through her. With a few inches to spare, she reached his flank and took a bite out of his side. Justin's wolf cried once more, thrashed, and stumbled. Her vision blurred. Needing a better grip, she let go and attacked again. Blood tinged her mouth as dizziness swamped her.

*Bite his neck.*

She didn't remember thinking it, but instinctively, she understood that was what she needed to do. Justin growled and batted a claw across her face, waking her up. Using the last of her reserve energy, Lexi sprang onto Justin's back. Instead of shaking her off, he rolled to the side and pinned her, but somehow, she still managed to sink her teeth into the side of his neck. Blood pooled rapidly, and the fight went out of him.

Pushing against him, she was able to get out from under his heavy body just as he took his last breath and transformed back into his human form.

Holy shit. She'd just killed Justin Kapok. Lexi had never killed anyone before, and while she was in shock at what she'd been capable of, she was elated that Sam would now be safe.

Sam! He better be okay.

She hobbled over to his prone form, trying to ignore the pain stabbing her. His chest rose and fell in shallow breaths as if his body was working hard to keep his heart pumping. His eyes were closed and his skin ashen. As much as she wanted to remain in her wolf form to fully heal, she had to shift in order to help him.

Lexi howled, hoping he'd be able to detect that she was near. Her jacket was only a few feet away as were her torn clothes. Her boots looked useable, but that was all that was salvageable. She'd be cold wearing only her down jacket, but she didn't want to leave Sam just to retrieve her spare outfit in the back of his truck. To be honest, she wasn't sure she could make it that far.

Standing next to her jacket, she shifted back to her human form and immediately pulled on her coat and stepped into the boots. Her coat was long enough to cover her butt but little of her legs. Her cell was in Sam's truck, but perhaps he had one on him. She picked up her ripped pants and returned to his side, her own breathing labored. Placing the ripped material on the ground, she knelt next to him.

"Sam, can you hear me?" She nudged him lightly. "Wake up."

When he didn't even groan, her heart lodged against her rib cage. With a shaky hand, she shoved her fingers into both of his coat pockets, but she didn't find his cell, only his keys. Pocketing them, she stood and searched his duffel, trying to ignore the racing ache between her neck and shoulder from the bite. Blood trickled down her back, the warm, sticky substance confirming that her energy was waning.

In the side pocket of the bag was his cell. Glory Be. Unless there was a GPS on this phone, she couldn't tell the ambulance where they were, as she didn't know exactly—other than to say it was near some caves. Even if they were able to find them, how would she explain to human paramedics about the naked man that was a few feet away with a large gash in his throat? The blood on her hands and face would be a dead giveaway that she'd killed him. She'd be in jail before Sam reached the hospital.

Jackson! He'd know what to do.

Sam said his friend had told him about this being a good place to target practice. Thankfully, everyone's number was pre-programmed in his cell so all she needed to do was press one button. Her thoughts clouded as she waited for Jackson to answer.

"Sam, how's shooting practice going?" he asked with a lot of cheer in his voice.

"Jackson. It's me, Lexi. Sam's been hurt." With as much calm as she could muster, she explained where they were and how several wolves had attacked him. "He's bleeding pretty badly."

"Can you put him on?"

"He's unconscious."

"Fuck. What about the rest of the wolves?"

"I killed Justin, and the others ran off."

"Stay there. I'll bring help."

With that he disconnected. Lexi gathered the rest of the torn clothing and then rolled Sam onto his side. Even though he was wearing his Pea Coat, the material in back was shredded and caked with blood. She pressed the fresh material over his cuts and then rolled him onto his back again, hoping the pressure would stem the flow. The icy ground should help with the swelling. Thinking it would take at least thirty minutes for Jackson to arrive with help, she rested her head on Sam's legs, hoping he could absorb some of her energy, what little she had left. She debated shifting to heal, but if he needed help, she wanted to be ready.

"Get away from him," a strangled voice sounded from about fifty feet away.

Lexi jerked her head up and blinked. She must be hallucinating. A woman, who looked a lot like Vinea was hovering several feet above the ground. She was dressed in a black gauze-like material that flowed about her body, and in her hand was some kind of crystal dagger. Between the tone and the knife, Lexi refused to do as she asked.

"No." Lexi managed to stand and then move between Vinea and Sam, but her heart was beating faster than a hummingbird's, and her energy was draining fast. "Stay away. He's hurt."

Vinea lowered herself to the ground and became less transparent. "Who's going to stop me? You think you can shift into your wolf and kill me like you did Justin? Look at you. You can barely stand up."

How did she know that she'd killed him? Okay, perhaps the dead body behind her gave her a clue. "I plan to try," she said, even if she had to use the last ounce of her strength to stop her.

"You are a little fool. I am a goddess who can destroy you with a flick of my finger."

Goddesses were supposed to be good, though most likely she was some magician if she could float and appear almost invisible. The woman who Devon helped in Vermont had to be bluffing.

Sam had told her that Naliana was the only goddess to have ever visited Silver Lake. This wasn't Naliana in disguise since Vinea looked about twenty-five, and Naliana was supposedly closer to sixty. "Show me."

"Showing you will kill you." Her lip curled, and her eyes turned almost black.

"I've already called for help. They'll be here any minute."

"Then I guess I don't have much time."

"Time for what?" Lexi stiffened. She had to stall for as long as possible until Jackson arrived. Whether he had any abilities to stave off a proclaimed goddess, she didn't know. "Vinea, why are you even here? Devon and everyone have all been really nice to you." She used her soft, cajoling voice that she often used with students who acted up in class.

She scowled. "That just means they are all fools."

Where was this hatred coming from? "Why do you want to hurt Sam? He's never done anything to you."

"Since you seem so fond of this young man, I'll let you in on a little secret. I had something stolen from me, and I want it back; plain and simple."

Nothing was plain or simple about theft. "The last person on earth to steal something would be Sam."

She waved a hand and chuckled, but it held no cheer. "Sam didn't do the stealing. My sister, Naliana, did, and the only way to fight her for what is rightfully mine is to regain more power."

Clearly, she was insane. Nothing she said made any sense, but Lexi would play along. "What power is rightfully yours?" Her legs were about to give way, but she had to stand tall against this woman.

"The ability to be the matchmaker for all shifters. To do that, I need to be able to control people's thoughts."

That was what Sam could do. Lexi glanced behind Vinea hoping to spot Jackson coming to their rescue, but not even a bird was in view. She needed to distract her, only how? "There already is a goddess who is in charge of doing that, or so I've been told."

"Naliana. Yes, but that was supposed to be *my* job, now please stand back. I wasn't planning on killing Sam or you, but I will if you don't let me have his powers."

"What good will they do you?" Lexi could guess, but if she could keep Vinea talking, she could figure out a way to take her down.

"You humans are so slow. I plan to fight my sister for my rightful place. Now stand back. This is my last warning." Vinea lifted the hand that contained a clear crystal dagger and moved so quickly Lexi didn't even see her move until she was inches from them.

She shoved Lexi. Losing her balance, she landed on her butt. Lexi had to shift. It was her only hope of saving Sam. Just as she was about to, an incredibly bright ray of light blasted Vinea, temporarily blinding Lexi.

"What are you doing here?" Vinea asked, her voice filled with hatred.

Lexi stopped the shift. As she opened her eyes, another ethereal creature appeared before them wearing a gossamer white gown. This newcomer was taller and thinner and had silver hair that rippled down her back. Despite the sheer outfit, the woman didn't look the least bit cold. While her skin was smooth, she looked to be in her sixties. This had to be Naliana.

"I'd like to ask you the same question," the older woman said with a stern voice tinged with disgust.

Vinea dropped the knife, and Lexi was tempted to grab it, but her muscles seemed to be frozen. She blinked and the newcomer materialized, looking fully human.

"I needed this man's power," Vinea announced as if stealing it was the most natural thing in the world. The slight fear in her voice had been replaced with arrogance.

"By cutting it out of him? I'm sorry the darkness had spread so deeply within you, but the light I just infused you with should help reverse that now."

Vinea's brows pinched, and her hands clenched, suddenly looking very human. "How does it make you feel to once more cheat me out of what is rightfully mine?"

Lexi didn't understand the conversation, but she was highly thankful to Naliana—if that was who she was—for stopping Vinea from taking Sam's power.

Sam moaned, and Lexi placed a hand on his heart, hoping her presence would help him stay calm. Right now these two women were focused on each other, which meant every minute that went by, Jackson had a better chance of arriving. Unfortunately, the addition of a few more wolves probably wouldn't bother a goddess or two.

The second woman moved closer. "Vinea, your actions of long ago caused the gods—not me—to ban you. In fact, I begged them to reconsider, but your own jealousy turned your heart too black. My wish was not granted because the gods were not pleased that I refused to visit them for so many years. Trust me, I didn't abandon you... You had to be sent to the dark realm."

What was she talking about? So Vinea really was a goddess? And what the hell was this dark realm place anyway?

"I happen to like it there, but by stripping me of my powers, I've been forced to continue my evil ways as you say, instead of making amends. It's why I need Sam's magic."

The second lady chuckled. "To do what? Get into my head? The gods would never allow it."

"We'll see."

"Obviously, you have no intention of repenting, but if you ever do want forgiveness, I'm sure we can find a way to make it happen."

"Forgiveness?" Vinea's brows furrowed and she planted a hand over her chest. "Oh, shit. What's wrong with me? What did you do?"

The second woman smiled. "It's the white light working on you. I wanted to help you before, but when you were banned, I couldn't follow to give you the light of goodness. With time, you'll want to do good by helping others."

Vinea looked around, her gaze falling on Sam. Goddess or not, Lexi would shift if she had to in order to protect the man she loved. An overwhelming need for him filled her. Yes, she loved Sam

Pompley, and no one was going to get near him. She'd die first.

Vinea whipped back toward the woman. "How are you even here? The white moon isn't for another few days. I planned it that way so you couldn't interfere."

"Oh, Vinea. You've been gone so long that you don't understand how things work in the light realm anymore. When the gods became aware of what you'd done, they gave me special compensation to return to earth—but only long enough to beg you to cease this crazy plan of yours."

Shouts sounded from the path below, and Lexi almost wept from joy. Jackson and one or two others had arrived. Naliana glanced in their direction.

"You need to decide what you want to do, Vinea. Get help, or you'll have to remain in the dark realm forever."

Vinea glanced at the path again. A second later Jackson, Connor, and Devon rushed onto the field.

It was as if Jackson and Connor didn't even see these women because they both ran over to Sam while Devon kept his focus on Vinea. Lexi couldn't read his expression, but from the way he was staring, he was in turmoil.

"What's going on, Vinea?" he asked, his voice nearly cracking.

"I'm being scolded by my younger sister. That's what's going on."

# Chapter Twenty-One

DEVON WAS IN total shock. His entire belief system had just been crushed. Upon seeing the two women, Jackson had whispered that the taller lady was the goddess Naliana. While Devon had never personally met her, he'd heard many tales. The first of which was that she only took her human form on the white moon, yet there wasn't one tonight. Did goddesses not have to adhere to the rules all of the time?

Why was Vinea even here, and what did she mean when she said her younger sister was scolding her?

"How can Naliana be your sister?" Devon asked as he moved closer.

Vinea sighed. "My poor Devon. I haven't been honest with you."

Her words took a moment to sink in. "Are you telling me you're a goddess?" Sure, she looked like one, but his body reacted as if she were his mate—as in a human mate.

"Yes, but I don't live where Naliana resides or rather where she floats about."

Her sister interjected. "Devon, I'm Naliana, and yes I am her younger sister. I'm sure Jackson and Connor have told you how I lived on earth for many years once I met James."

"They did."

"Because of my stay, I aged while Vinea did so very slowly. Vinea and I had to part ways many years ago. It was one of the reasons why

I couldn't face returning to the light realm for so long. That and I wanted to be with James. You see, Vinea was so jealous of me for being designated as the shifter matchmaker that she was stripped of most of her powers and sent to the dark realm to repent." Naliana glanced over at her sister. "I'm sad to say she's failed at changing her ways. However, I still have hope that she can redeem herself—with help."

With help? "I don't understand."

"It might be best for now, that you don't. It will take a while for most of her evil spirit to dissipate."

That explanation didn't help at all. Needing to touch Vinea, possibly to believe she was real and not some illusion, he drew closer.

Vinea held up a hand. "Don't, please, Devon. This is equally hard for me to understand. Right now, I can feel my body changing, and I hate it."

"Changing?" She wasn't a shifter. "I just want to touch you." Okay, that sounded creepy, but his wolf was going crazy around her.

*Stand down. This woman is evil*, he told his animal.

"I need to go," she said.

"No, wait. I have to talk to you."

Ignoring him, she rushed toward the woods, but before she reached the tree line, her figure became faint and then disappeared completely. What the hell? He needed answers. What happened just now had been wrong—so terribly wrong.

"Devon, give us a hand," Connor called, acting as if Vinea hadn't just been there.

Shit. He'd come to help Sam, not touch base with the woman who'd haunted his dreams. "Coming," he replied then faced Naliana once more. "Please help me understand."

"My time here is up, but I will give you this piece of advice: Be patient."

With that, she moved backward then floated above the ground. Her image faded and then disappeared into nothingness just like her sister before her.

"Devon!" Connor called.

He jerked his attention to the two men who'd placed Sam on the canvas cot. He rushed to them, pushing aside his confusion and frustration. "Where do you need me?"

"Grab one of the front handles, as all the weight will be at that end when we head downhill."

"Let me grab his bag too," Devon said. Lexi was on her feet, but she was swaying. Devon placed a hand on her back. "You need to shift."

"I'll be okay."

Her lips had already turned blue. With her legs bare, the poor woman had to be freezing. It appeared as if she'd shifted to fight Justin Kapok who now lay bloodied and naked twenty feet away. His admiration for her grew even more.

"Please."

She looked over at Jackson and Connor who were waiting for her before they picked up the stretcher with Sam on it. "All right," she said.

Lexi slipped off her coat and stepped out of her shoes. A few seconds later, she was in her wolf form. Devon shoved her gear into the bag then lifted her wolf and placed her on top of Sam's legs. He figured it would do both of them some good to be near each other.

For the next half hour, they carefully carried Sam down to Jackson's truck, hurrying yet trying to be careful not to jar him too much.

"Put him in the back," Jackson said as he handed Connor the keys. "I'm going back to take care of Kapok. You take Sam back to the office. I'll meet you there."

"I'll drive Sam's truck back," Devon said. "Can you find his keys?"

Jackson dug his hand into Sam's pockets. "Not there."

Devon searched Lexi's coat pocket. "Got 'em."

He opened the backseat and Lexi jumped in. He was pleased she appeared more energetic. The half hour rest had done wonders for her. Devon followed Connor back to the office, hoping Sam would be okay.

LEXI HAD TOO many questions to ask to remain in her wolf form. Besides, the rest down the mountain had allowed her wolf to heal her quite well. Keeping low, she shifted in the backseat. "Brr."

"Welcome back," Devon said. "I'll turn up the heat. I put your coat and shoes in the bag."

"Thanks." She pulled them out and then shoved her arms in her jacket and stuffed her feet in her boots.

"Want to tell me what happened?" Devon asked.

She explained about them going out there for target practice. "As I was taking a bathroom break in the woods, Sam's yells and the wolves' cries had me racing back to help. Two wolves were clawing at him when another two showed up. Then Justin appeared."

"Sam was being attacked by four wolves? I'm surprised he lived."

"The second two were watching. I was about to shift and help him when Justin appeared. When he saw me, he called off all of the wolves."

"Why would he do that?"

"I think he was trying to get my attention. He succeeded. Justin told me that if I didn't go back to Vermont with him that he'd give the order for his men to kill Sam." Her voice shook retelling the story. "By then Sam had collapsed. I could tell the wolves could have killed him easily, and I couldn't have stopped them all."

"But you didn't go with Justin."

"No. I thought I could bluff my way out of it. I told Justin that Sam and I were already mated, but he didn't believe me because he'd bugged our truck."

Devon shot her a look. "Oh, shit. You mean this truck is bugged?"

She'd forgotten about that. "Yes."

"Once we have Sam stabilized, I'll check it out."

"We know Justin can't listen in since he's dead, but yes, take it out by all means."

Devon didn't ask any more questions, probably because some of Justin's men might be listening. It wasn't long before the McKinnon and Associates office came into view, and Lexi's anxieties shot up once more. Devon pulled to a stop behind Connor, cut the engine, and handed her Sam's keys. "Don't worry."

Like that would ever happen? He jumped out, and she followed. Cold air blasted her, but her heart was beating so fast that she barely noticed. As much as she wanted to run up to Sam, she didn't want to impede their progress. Connor swiped his thumb on the keyless entry, and Lexi held open the back door for them. Once inside, she followed them to the infirmary.

Sam held out his hand, and she clasped it. His skin was pale, and he struggled to talk. "I love you."

"I love you too. Don't talk, just concentrate on getting better."

Sam's eyes rolled back in his head, and Connor touched her arm. "I've called Missy and she'll be here soon. Go clean up and put on something warm. I imagine you'll be sitting with him for a while."

"I will." She figured he mostly wanted her out of the way so Missy could do her magic.

Lexi rushed to Devon's office where she disappeared behind the bookcase. Sam was alive, and that was all that mattered. In the moments when he was lying in the field, the life draining out of him, her own life had passed before her eyes. His importance had become solidified in each and every cell of her body. She made a promise: as soon as Sam healed, she'd make things permanent. Justin Kapok was dead, and the men and women of Silver Lake had become her family.

Would she miss Ronan and her friends back in Vermont? Sure, but she'd made new friends here, though she might be able to convince her brother to visit. Who knows? He might fall in love with the town just as she had.

Still chilled to the bone, Lexi turned on the shower, and only after the water warmed did she remove her jacket and boots. Her legs, she feared, might stay frozen for life. The first dip hurt, but as soon as she warmed, she sighed from the relief. As much as she wanted to stand under the heated stream for an hour, Sam was upstairs, and she was a firm believer in giving support. If she'd been injured, just having him there would have helped her heal.

Once Lexi was positive none of Justin's blood was still on her, she stepped out of the shower and dried off. A few scrapes and cuts still marred her body, but most of the deep ones had healed. Thank goodness for her wolf.

After pulling on a comfy sweatshirt, her baggiest jeans, a pair of thick socks, and sneakers, she rushed upstairs. When she stepped into their infirmary, Missy had lit candles and incense and placed them around Sam's bed. She twisted around to face her.

"Lexi!"

"Hey, Missy. How's Sam?"

"Doing better. I put a poultice on his back and then placed some herbs under his head. He might need stitches, and because we don't need the authorities questioning you about wolves, you should have a shifter doctor look at him if he isn't better by tomorrow. The last thing you need is a manhunt for these wolves."

Lexi shivered. "That would be bad."

Sam opened his eyes and reached out for her hand. "Lexi?" His voice sounded weak.

"I'm right here."

Missy picked up her flowered bag and slung it over her shoulder. "Make sure to blow out the candles when they get low. Call me tomorrow if he needs another dose of magic."

Lexi hugged Missy. "Thank you so much."

"You're welcome, but I was born with this ability to heal. It's what I need to do."

Once she left, Lexi pulled up a chair next to his bed. "How are you feeling—really?"

"Better."

"Tell me what you remember," she said.

"I was putting the guns in the bag when two wolves came up behind me and attacked. Otherwise, I would have stopped them. Even though I was in a fight for my life, when the second pair arrived, I convinced them to wait. Sneak attacks have always been an issue for me."

"If you were a shifter, you'd have been able to detect them."

"True, but I'm not one."

She smiled. "If you play your cards right, you could be."

Sam chuckled. "Then I better heal fast. What happened to Kapok?"

"After he told his men to leave you alone, he insisted I go with him. That's when I shifted and attacked Justin. Thankfully, the wolves didn't seem to care. They just trotted off. I'm guessing you suggested they go?"

"Yes. Thankfully, they listened and didn't try to help Justin take you down."

She shivered. She'd have been killed for sure. Not wanting to think about it, she refocused her attention on Sam's injuries. "How about you roll over? I want to check those gouge marks on your back?"

"Did you get your medical degree while I was out cold?"

She huffed out a laugh. "No, but I'll sleep better if I know you're healing."

"Fine, but I really am feeling better. I don't know what Missy did, but whatever it was, it seems to be working."

When Sam rolled over and winced, it hurt her to see him in pain. Once on his stomach, she lifted his bloodstained shirt, but Missy had put bandages over the wounds. "I don't want to remove the bandages. How about you sleep on your stomach for tonight?"

"I think you're right."

If Lexi had been seriously injured and in pain like Sam was, she might want something strong to drink. "Is there any liquor in this place?"

"Can't handle the sight of blood?" he asked.

Silly man. "I thought you'd like a stiff drink."

"I could use one. Ask Devon or Connor. They usually stash a bottle someplace."

Lexi stood. "I'll be right back."

She hurried out in search of one of the men. Devon's door was the first one she came to, so she knocked and entered.

"Hey, how is he?" Devon asked.

"I can't inspect his wounds since they're covered, but he's in good spirits."

"He'll be fine then."

"While Sam won't say so, I could see it in his face that he's in some pain. Do you have any liquor I can give him?"

Devon smiled. "I sure do. Dad likes to keep bottles around." He opened his desk drawer and retrieved a bottle of Scotch along with a glass. "I don't offer this to just anyone, but this is for a good cause."

"Thanks. One or two shots of this and he'll be out all night."

"I agree. Oh, by the way, I found the listening device in Sam's truck. It's the same one I gave Vinea. There are seven more, and I'll keep looking until I find them."

"I wouldn't be surprised if she bugged Sam's house." How else had she learned where she and Sam would be?

"I agree. Vinea was a horrible person."

"I'm sorry. I believed her story too. I still find it hard to believe she's a goddess."

"I can't wrap my head around it either. I'm such an idiot. I fell for her helpless act hook, line, and sinker."

From his thinned lips and the way his gaze was darting around, Devon was majorly upset. "It could happen to anyone. You're a protector, and that's what protectors do. You couldn't have known. Being fooled by a goddess isn't shameful."

"Tell that to my ego."

Devon was being hard on himself. And then it occurred to her. "You really liked her, didn't you?"

His face flushed. "Kind of, though obviously I didn't know her like I thought I did."

"So now what?"

"Now? Nothing. You saw what kind of person Vinea is. I just hope that she goes back to where she belongs and never returns."

"That's probably for the best. Did you know she was about to stab Sam in the chest with a knife right before you guys showed up?"

"What?"

Devon deserved to know the truth. "Vinea planned to steal his powers. Naliana showed up and stopped her. I was about to shift, but in truth, even if I hadn't been injured, I don't think I could have stopped a goddess."

"Motherfucker. Well this sucks."

Lexi agreed. From his outburst, Vinea had meant something to him. "Thank goodness she's gone for now. I'm not sure what Naliana did to her, but it seems as if that light she infused her with altered her somehow."

He nodded. "I don't care. I never want to see her again."

She'd never heard such bitterness. Lexi lifted the bottle and shot glass. "Thanks for this."

"Take good care of him."

"I will."

When Lexi arrived back at the infirmary, Sam was sound asleep so she set down the bottle and glass. While she was tempted to drink some herself, she decided against it as the twinges in her shoulder were slowly subsiding, and if Sam needed her, she wanted to be able to react.

Lexi stretched out her legs to settle in for a long night. Sam's legs would occasionally jerk and then he would moan but quickly fall back to sleep. Lexi closed her eyes and hoped that by morning, Missy's magic had worked a miracle on Sam.

# Chapter Twenty-Two

WHEN SAM OPENED his eyes, it took him a moment to realize where he was. The dull thudding ache in his back prompted him to recall the fight, or rather the attack. He was eternally grateful that the wolves had come after him instead of Lexi. If she'd been injured, he'd be a complete mess by now, even though her wolf could have healed her quickly.

Moving slowly, he rolled over and was pleased the pain wasn't as bad as it had been last night. His heart warmed seeing Lexi slumped over in the chair, her soft snores a soothing sound to his ears. As if she sensed he'd awoken, Lexi jerked and opened her eyes.

She smiled and sat up. "Good morning. How are you feeling?"

"Fine." She had on the same jeans and top that she'd put on yesterday. "Did you spend the night here?"

"Yes. I was worried you might take a turn for the worse."

"You didn't have to do that." To show her he was good, he pushed up on his elbows.

"Yes I did, now rest," she begged.

He flexed his back, and the bandage seemed to be stuck to him. Sam yanked off the covers. "I need to shower and wash the blood off me. Care to help?"

"Why don't you roll over and I'll check you out first? I don't want you to make things worse."

He chuckled. "That's just a ploy. I know you. You don't think you can control yourself if I'm naked."

She huffed. "My control is not the issue here. To be honest, I'm worried about you. If you're still wounded, my common sense will trump my libido."

He laughed, loving how his woman thought. He stretched and actually felt quite good. Placing his feet on the floor, he stood. His balance faltered for a second, but after a moment, he steadied. "The gauze will come off easier in the shower. You ready to escort me to your humble abode downstairs?"

Her mouth opened. "I will, but I just realized now that I'm no longer at risk, I'll be able to leave the safe house."

Sam stepped close and wrapped his arms around her. "That's great. You can move in with me."

Her eyes sparkled. "For real?"

"For real." Sam still couldn't believe how lucky he'd been to find such a wonderful woman. "I want to check you out too. I'm sure Kapok got in a few licks before you took him down."

"I'm fine."

"You'll have to prove it to me."

"You see? You want to get me naked too."

Sam grinned. "Caught me."

Devon wasn't in his office as they passed through the space to reach the hidden staircase, for which he was glad. He didn't need someone else telling him to rest. Once they arrived in the suite, Sam stepped into the bathroom, anxious to clean up. Dried blood was nasty.

"Do you need help undressing?" she asked.

No man in his right mind would say no. "Sure."

He turned on the water then faced Lexi. He wasn't wearing shoes, but he was dressed in the same attire as when the wolves had attacked him. He didn't even want to think about what his favorite jacket looked like. Most likely one of the men had tossed it, which was just as well. Sam would have had trouble parting with it. That jacket and he had been through a lot.

Lexi stepped in front of him and slowly lifted his shirt. He almost felt bad after raising his arms, as even he could smell himself. She however didn't react. Once she removed his shirt, she turned him around so that his back was facing her.

"How does it look?" he asked.

"I really can't tell until the bandages come off, and I'm afraid to remove them. I don't want to open the cuts up."

"Let's let the shower do its magic." Being so close to Lexi was messing with his head. Her touch was already sending him to another place. As fast as he could, he ditched his pants and briefs. He wasn't sure he could handle it if she touched him intimately.

When he turned around, she smiled and nodded at his cock. "By your stiffness, you can't be too injured."

"It always works like that when I'm around you."

She chuckled. "Get in while I undress."

Either she must not think her wounds were bad or she didn't want to let him check her out. He dunked his head under the warm spray and moaned at the luxurious feeling. When the water streamed down his back, it stung, but not bad enough to worry about needing any stitches. Through the glass shower door, he watched her undress as he soaped up.

Lexi was quick, and soon she was standing next to him. "Do you want me to peel off the bandages?" Now that they were wet, he'd have to change them anyway.

"Sure." With care, she took them off. He half expected her to gasp when she saw the raw skin, but she didn't. When she lightly ran her hand down his back, she didn't hit anything sensitive.

"Well?" He had high hopes.

"I think you are a shifter already. Your ability to heal is amazing. It's still red, but the cuts have mostly closed." From the shower stall, she tossed the bandages into the trashcan.

Sam twisted around and instantly shot his gaze to her neck region. "You're looking good yourself."

She placed a hand over an area that was still red. "My wolf did all the work."

Sam drew her into an embrace and kissed her, and he swore he could almost feel her love rushing through him and making him whole again. As much as he didn't want to stop, he did need to finish washing.

He broke the kiss and handed her the soap. "You want to do the honors?"

"My pleasure." Her look meant trouble.

With great care, she washed his back before moving down to his legs. Her touch set his body on fire, but he remained still, wanting her to be convinced that he was in good enough shape to make love to her. Lexi and he belonged together, forever.

He spent his life making sure others remained safe, but he had to admit that having Lexi at his side was comforting.

Sam spun around. "Other side."

"This will be fun." She started washing his chest then his arms. Sparks coming from both of them pinged off the shower walls, and when she glanced down, his cock throbbed. "I think I forgot something."

"Damn straight. The most important part." He thought he'd be able to handle the stimulation, but he was wrong. After three pumps, he grabbed her hand. "Enough."

Sam turned off the water and opened the shower door.

"What's wrong? Did I squeeze too tight?" Lexi looked up at him with eyes that screamed *Take Me*.

"Yes, you did, which means you need to make amends. Go on. Dry off."

They both stepped out of the shower and then grabbed towels. He tried to dry her off while she swiped the towel over his body. Their hands collided, and soon, Sam decided to take her the way she was—wet tits and all. He tossed his towel on the floor and led her to the bed. While his back was healing, he figured Lexi would worry less if she were lying on the mattress instead of him. In one quick swoop, he picked her up and deposited her on the bed.

"Now for my feast," he announced.

Lexi held up her hands and glanced down at his dick. "Me first."

"Dear goddess in heaven. You know what will happen."

She grinned. "I'll be quick. My wolf is having a hard time staying put. Can you kneel for me?"

Sam positioned himself, readying for the intensive sexual stimulation. Lexi grabbed his hard shaft, leaned over, and devoured his cock. He latched onto her shoulders, careful not to squeeze too hard. His blue aura glowed and pulsed with each suck of her mouth. It was as if she was helping him transcend to the light realm. Not intending to release this fast, a burst of cum shot out. Damn. He thought he'd be able to keep in control, but Lexi's scent and amazing technique threw him off kilter.

*I love her with my whole heart. That's why I have no control.*

His love overwhelmed his willpower. "My turn," he said, not sure he could keep from fully coming.

She stuck out her tongue and dropped back onto the bed. Sam eased between her legs, anxious to take her to new heights. She tasted so fucking good that the first lick had him reeling. When he slipped a finger into her opening, Lexi groaned and arched her back.

"I'm ready now, Sam."

He loved when she begged. "Just a little more."

Having her desperate excited him. He returned to flicking her little nub. With his free hand, he reached up and kneaded her breast, and the combination had his dick harder than steel. When he pressed on the most sensitive spot inside, her bones began to crack.

"Sam!"

The loud plea had him sitting up. Fur flew and she spun right before him. A second later, she was in her wolf form. Oh, holy shit. "Lexi?"

She moved closer, and he held out his hand. She licked his palm then leaped off the bed. More fur spun and bones cracked again. A second later, she was standing in front of him in her beautifully naked human form.

"I am so sorry. I was so turned on that my wolf escaped."

"Really?" He'd never had a woman do that before. "You ready for some more?"

She laughed as she crawled back on to the bed. "I can't promise it won't happen again, so you better hurry."

Being on edge, himself, he had no problem obliging. As soon as Sam crawled on top of her, the skin-to-skin contact nearly made him come right then. Grabbing his shoulders, she dragged him down. Their lips touched and he slid right into her.

LEXI NEARLY LOST it again. Her wolf howled and her body swam with endorphins. Sam was everything she'd ever wanted, so the urge to bite him nearly overwhelmed her, but she wanted to wait to give him time to fully enjoy this momentous occasion. Tonight they would mate and start their life together.

"Kiss me," he whispered.

Lexi pulled his head to hers and kissed him with every ounce of passion in her body. Sam swept his tongue around hers and drove his hard cock into her. Holy mother of gods. Even if her wolf was able to contain herself, Lexi wasn't sure she could. Not wanting to chance hurting his back, she threaded her fingers through his hair and hung on tight. Pressing her feet onto the mattress, she met each and every one of his thrusts with ones of her own.

His musky scent overwhelmed her, and her climax teetered on the edge. His groans and moans altered something inside her, and when he thrust in hard and then held still, she could no longer keep from claiming him.

She broke the kiss just as her teeth sharpened to a point. While the hair on her arms was usually faint, new coarser hair was poking through. Not able to wait any longer, she lowered her mouth to his neck and dug her teeth in. That first taste caused her glow to enlarge so much that it melded with his. A startling white light arced between them, creating a connection so deep that not only did she climax, her body seemed to absorb his essence.

Sam's cock exploded a second later, and he held her tight, like he never wanted to let her go. Time stood still as pure love entered her body. Her mind spun, and her vision blurred. Lexi couldn't say how many minutes went by until Sam eventually rolled onto his side.

"I've never experienced anything like that before," he said, his voice filled with awe.

"Me neither."

He dragged a knuckle down her cheek. "What happens next?"

She was pretty sure he'd heard all about the physical changes that would occur, from the telepathy between mates, to him being able to now shift into a wolf. "We live happily ever after?"

"I'm willing," he said.

So was she. He laughed then kissed her again. In no time they were ready for a repeat performance of the most amazing night of her life.

# Chapter Twenty-Three

S AM CUT THE engine to his truck and parked at the base of the hiking path that led up to where he'd taught Lexi how to shoot. It didn't matter that he'd watched her transform into a wolf many times, not to mention the men he worked with who changed into bears and even tigers. Him undergoing this transformation was hard to believe. Not that he'd been jealous of what the other men had been able to do, but he had always wondered what it would be like.

"Are you nervous?" Lexi asked.

It might not be macho to admit it, but he never wanted to keep a secret from her. "A little."

"I'm excited to see you in your wolf form."

He chuckled. "You would be."

She patted his shoulder then opened the truck door. "Let's go."

This was it. The evening was clear and the moon was full. He slipped out of the truck, and together they hiked up the hill. By the time they'd reached the relatively flat field, he was warm. Lexi had suggested they return here. Perhaps it was to convince herself that living on the run was finally over and that Justin Kapok was really dead.

Sam, however, would have been happy never to go there again as that hadn't been his finest moment. He was a trained soldier and should have put up a better fight.

"Ready to get naked?" Lexi said with a smile.

"I'm always ready to take off my clothes around you, but this time it won't be for the purpose of making love. I'm slightly warm from hiking up here, but it's still damned cold."

She laughed. "I promise you'll warm up quickly once you start running."

"What if I can't change?" This was the real reason for his concern.

"Why would you say that? Elana told me it was easy."

He grunted. "For her maybe, but not for her brother. Brian spent a good month trying. If Jillian hadn't been in trouble, he might never have accomplished it."

She lifted her arms around his neck. "Are you afraid?"

"If you think that, then you don't know me very well. It's just that I've already had one failure in this spot. I don't need another."

She kissed his lips lightly. "Having several wolves attack you and live to tell about it can never be considered a failure. Remember what happened to Jackson?"

"Yes. He was in his bear form and nearly died after four wolves attacked him."

"Right and you battled two as a human and lived."

"If Justin hadn't called off his men, I might not have survived."

She stepped away. "But he did. End of discussion. Let's leave our clothes by the big tree over there." She trotted over, and he followed. "I wonder if we'll be able to communicate telepathically once you shift?" she asked as she slipped off her jacket.

He'd spoken to Jackson about it. He said that as soon as he and Ainsley had mated, they'd been able to communicate. But since Sam couldn't get into Lexi's head before they mated, he suspected he wouldn't be able to afterward. His grandfather might have been right: Wendayans with his talent couldn't make the telepathic link with their mate. That was okay. Being able to shift would make up for it. What he did hope for was that if Lexi were ever in trouble that he'd be able to sense her need.

"Sam? The link?" she asked.

"Oh, sorry. It's possible, but I'm tending more toward no."

She smiled. "We'll figure it out. Now strip."

He laughed. He did love his woman. Once he ditched his clothes, he wanted to get moving. "So I just think about being a wolf?"

"I thought you asked Jackson."

"I did, but Ainsley was already a shifter, and Kip doesn't shift." Now he wished he'd spoken to Elana, Izzy, or Anna.

"Just follow me. When I shift, you should too. I hope."

"Go!"

Lexi took off. While he had excellent eyesight for a human, it wasn't nearly as good as Lexi's. If he tripped, he'd never forgive himself. She sprinted, and he followed as closely behind as possible.

As smoothly as could be, Lexi seemed to swirl and then transform into her wolf form, but he couldn't. He was still running on two legs. Failure smacked him in the face.

*Think like a wolf. Clear away all negative thoughts.* The last thought had been what his grandfather had always told him about focusing on a goal.

*You can do it.* Sam swore it sounded like the old man's voice.

A strong ache began in his chest and raced through his body. The sky turned even darker, despite the white moon streaming its light across the field. He couldn't see for a few seconds and then a tight band squeezed around his chest. Just as he thought he was falling, his hands met the ground and then his vision cleared.

His gate changed, and his hands weren't hands at all, but rather furry paws. He'd shifted! Sam couldn't believe it. A wave of joy spread through him as he raced to follow Lexi. She'd reached the end of the field and turned left to follow the tree line. His wolf was bigger than hers, and in seconds he'd caught up with her.

*"It's fantastic."* He sent the message in his head.

*"It sure is!*

He couldn't believe they could communicate. Wanting to share the joy, he leapt into the air, thrilled how his body could respond so quickly to each command. If he could climb a tree, he would have.

Lexi turned toward the middle of the field, and he raced right alongside her. When she reached the middle, she slowed.

Curious what she was about to do, he drew up next to her. Lexi sniffed his face and then pawed the air, acting as if she wanted to play. He was game. Showing her he understood, he dropped to the ground and she pounced. All in the spirit of play, he batted away her attack, and she ducked from his. He had to admit, she was quite good at avoiding his paws. They rolled on the ground that was dotted with random patches of snow. He'd nip at her. She'd nip at him.

Then in a flash, Lexi jumped off him and ran toward the line of trees where they had left their clothes. Sam chased after her and almost caught up with her just as she stopped. Her fur flew and then she was back to her human form.

"Brr. Better shift back, unless you want me to drive you home in your wolf form." She laughed.

How did he do that? Sam closed his eyes to better focus. Seeing her naked destroyed his ability to do anything. His body shook and his vision turned black. Cold sliced through his body. When he regained his ability to think, he was on his hands and knees, and Lexi was clapping.

"Good job, if not rather unorthodox."

"Unorthodox, huh? You could have told me how to return to my human form."

She handed him his clothes. "Sorry. I completely forgot about that part. So what did you think?" she asked.

Sam donned his clothes. "Being a wolf was so much better than I ever imagined. The freedom to run that fast was astounding."

"Yay! I'm so glad you like it. There is nothing as exhilarating than being able to let loose." She slipped on her jacket. "The most exciting thing was being able to communicate telepathically."

*"It was amazing. I guess my grandfather was wrong. Come here."* He was excited to learn if she could understand him now that he wasn't in his shifted form. But Lexi didn't move or act as if she could

hear him. "Lexi, did you hear what I just telepathed to you?"

"No."

"Maybe our telepathic link only works when we are in our animal form."

She moved closer and wrapped her arms around his neck. "I don't mind. Being able to communicate in our animal form works for me."

"Me too." He held her tight. "What do you say we head back? Maybe after I show you how much I appreciate you, we can work on your newfound talent," Sam said. "But you have to promise not to use it on unsuspecting people."

She smiled. "I promise only to warp the minds of evil people. But to practice, won't we need someone else? I can't practice on you."

He grinned. "That's true, but for now, I want to keep you all to myself!"

*Two months later*

SAM PARKED A half a block away from Kalan and Elana's house. "I didn't know so many people wanted to go to a one-year old's birthday party," Sam said.

"Aiden is so cute and such a charmer. Everyone just loves him."

"True. Do you want to have children?" Sam asked.

"I most certainly do, but I want us to wait a bit. I want you all to myself for at least a year."

He cut the engine. "Only a year?"

Lexi laughed. "You know what I mean. You're going to be a great father, and you'll want to spend time with your son or daughter."

"Son." He pushed open his door and came over to her side.

Lexi would be happy with any child. She grabbed Aiden's present, and together they headed toward the house. All the snow had melted, and she was looking forward to spring. Noise filtered through the front window of the house.

Sam didn't even knock. He pressed the latch and went in. Helium balloons littered the room. Izzy and Anna were on the sofa next to each other. Izzy, who was five months pregnant, was holding Aiden and blowing in his face, making him laugh. Anna was seven months along and looked as if she was going to have twins she was so big. Elana was in the kitchen, and Kalan was with Rye and Connor.

"I think half the town is here," Sam said.

"It sure looks like it. I wish Devon didn't have to go back to Pennsylvania. I've grown fond of him."

"Well, he does run that office."

"I know."

The doorbell rang and a second later Brian and Jillian came in. He was carrying what looked like a scooter. Right behind him was Jackson with Ainsley.

Since she'd arrived in town, Sam had worked hard to make sure Lexi met as many of his friends as possible. Given she was both a Wendayan and a shifter, she belonged to both groups.

Elana clapped her hands, and they all turned toward her. "I want to thank everyone for coming to Aiden's first birthday. I can't believe how fast this year has gone by. It seems like only yesterday that we were all over at Kip and Teagan's house watching Sam do his magic on Missy, and then Jillian had to rush me to the hospital after Aiden stopped breathing."

"Uh, you stopped breathing too, if you recall correctly," Jillian added.

"A mother's reaction to her distressed son." The group laughed. "Now that my brother has arrived—late as usual—how about we open the presents?"

"Hey, I had to make sure the paint was dry," Brian said, but she could tell he enjoyed the banter.

The men dragged the dining room chairs to living room for more seating. Elana lifted the baby from Izzy's arms and took the chair across from her. One by one, she opened the presents. Of course, Aiden was enthralled, mostly with the wrapping paper. The presents varied from clothing to toys. She and Sam had brought him a large stuffed wolf.

When Brian handed her his gift, her eyes watered. "It's wonderful."

"Let me show him how to use it." Brian lifted his nephew from her arms and placed Aiden in the round seat. Immediately, Aiden began to pump his little legs and he scooted across the floor. The baby squealed in delight.

Sam reached over and squeezed Lexi's hand. The love and support in this room was healing most of the hurt in her life, and she couldn't be happier.

With so many people in the room, Aiden couldn't get too far, but Elana retrieved her son nonetheless. He screamed for a moment until she waved something shiny in front of his face and he immediately calmed. Then they finished opening the rest of the presents.

Sam leaned over to Lexi. "Would you mind if I make the announcement now?"

Lexi hadn't been sure if she wanted to take away from Aiden's big day, but the baby was totally enthralled with his new gifts, and Elana looked so content. In truth, Lexi wasn't sure she could keep the news to herself any longer. From the way Teagan was glancing over at both of them, she might spill the beans first. "Sure."

Sam stood. "We have an announcement."

The group quieted—everyone that is but Aiden.

Sam helped her up and then wrapped an arm around Lexi's waist. "Last week," he said, "Lexi and I flew down to Florida again. While it was true that it was my Dad's sixtieth birthday, when we arrived, we decided to do something very human."

The crowd seemed to think about his words, and then Missy piped up. "You got married, didn't you?"

Lexi couldn't contain herself any longer. "Yes! Since Teagan and Kip were there for the birthday celebration, we thought we'd head to the courthouse and make it official." She lifted her hand to show everyone her ring, which had a large white diamond in the middle with two smaller black onyx stones on either side. Sam said those two represented their wolves.

The women rushed over to her, and the men slapped Sam on the back.

"Let me see," Missy said. "It's beautiful. I'm so happy for you."

Hugs went all around. Rye tapped his glass and held it up. "Here's to the new additions to our Clan. Welcome."

Being part of a loving Clan as wonderful as this one in Silver Lake, as well as being mated with Sam, was a dream come true.

"Thank you," Sam said. "It means the world to me to have the most amazing woman for my mate."

Everyone clapped and cheered. Life was so good.

## The End

*Don't forget to sign up for my newsletter to receive three free books, as well as up-to-date information on my stories. If you prefer to only receive notices regarding my releases, follow me on BookBub.*
http://smarturl.it/o4cz93?IQid=MLite
bookbub.com/authors/vella-day

I hoped you enjoyed Sam and Lexi's story. Up next is Missy and Zane's story (a newcomer to the series), WAKING HER BEAR. Here's the first chapter.

# Chapter One

MISSY BERTA RUSHED out of the Crystal Winds Spa in need of some herbs to help heal her good friend, Anna Fairchild, who was expecting her first child next month. Anna had come down with a fever, and while Missy knew just what she needed to help her and her baby, only one of the two required ingredients was readily available. Natalie Fremont, the owner of the local herb store carried the ginger root but not the Reishi mushrooms, and the only place to get those was south of town near the caves. Not wanting to waste any time, Missy gathered her herb bag and headed out of town.

Thankfully her mom and her cousin Teagan told her they would cover for her while she went on her search of the needed medicine. No one questioned the fact that Anna's health came first.

Once in the car, Missy rolled down the windows to breathe in the fresh May air, willing her pulse to slow. She was confident her magic could help Anna, but only if she could find the precise ingredients.

Normally the beginning of summer in Tennessee was Missy's favorite time of year, but her worry over Anna's condition tainted her joy. The sunshine, the chirping birds, and the scent from the new blooms of flowers always centered her, but not today. Something besides Anna's illness was bothering her, but Missy couldn't put her finger on what that was. For some reason, she was experiencing a sense of impending doom. Missy didn't usually have premonitions. That honor belonged to Teagan, but nonetheless Missy's nerves were jittery today.

When she reached the entrance to the hillside where the caves were located, she cut the engine, grabbed her canvas bag, and jumped out. She probably should have stopped at home for her hiking boots, but she wouldn't be climbing the hill for more than half a mile and her sandals would be sufficient for the short trek. Besides, time was of the essence.

With her herb kit slung over her shoulder, she began the journey up the rocky mountain trail. By the time she reached the peek, her sense of foreboding no longer had a tight grip on her emotions.

She'd often located these mushrooms in a cave that was only a short walk along the ridgeline. Needing a drink of water before she proceeded on the last leg of her journey, she pulled out her bottle and drank half of the contents. After returning her bottle to her bag she hurried along the path. Between the ginger, the mushrooms, and her magic, Missy was certain she could bring down Anna's fever without harming the baby.

The vista of Silver Lake never failed to stun her in its beauty, but today she didn't have the luxury of admiring the view. Finding the mushrooms had to be her top priority.

Near the mouth of the caves, she spotted a clump of Reishi mushrooms, and Missy mentally pumped a fist. She picked them quickly, and the relief at finding at least these few helped settled her nerves further. Unfortunately, she needed a lot more to make the right strength potion.

Hurrying, Missy located the three-foot wide cave entrance without any problem, but as soon as she stepped inside, a strange vibration rattled her bones. Respecting her sixth sense, she stopped and looked around. Anticipation and a sense of unease battled for her attention.

Her heart beat way too fast and that was never a good thing. "Hello? Is anyone here?" she called, her voice a little shaky.

Missy had never encountered anyone in this cave before, but it wasn't out of the realm of possibility that someone might be there. In bad weather, campers often sought refuge inside, but perhaps this summer day had brought out two lovers who wanted some privacy.

When no one answered, Missy figured it was her imagination. Retrieving her flashlight from her bag, she flicked in on, expecting the tightness in her body to release, but it didn't. Most likely, she was just worried about finding enough mushrooms.

Swinging the light around, she searched for her prize, but nothing appeared to be in the main entrance area. That meant she'd have to continue deeper into the caves. It wasn't that she feared something bad would happen to her, but it was always possible a wild animal might have decided to seek the coolness of the caves and attack if she scared him. Thankfully, part of Missy's Wendayan powers included exuding an aura of safety that seemed to calm even the most outraged beings.

Careful not to trip on any protruding rocks, Missy did a slow grid search to make sure she didn't miss any of the much-needed fungi.

Aha! Luck was on her side. About a hundred feet in, she spotted what she'd been searching for. Thrilled her search had been short, she squatted down and carefully pinched off the caps then placed them in a plastic bag. She'd extracted about ten of them when a growl came from deep inside the cave. From the low tone, it was most likely a bear. While a bear shifter wasn't a threat, a real bear with cubs would be.

Holding her breath in order to distinguish her heartbeat from what she thought was a wild animal, Missy remained still and listened for sounds of movement. Even though she detected nothing, she decided she had enough mushrooms to make the potion for Anna. Careful not to make any noise, Missy rose. While she probably could calm even a mother bear, she didn't want to test her theory. Turning off her light so as not to attract more attention, she twisted around and headed toward the entrance. In the near dark cave, she stepped on a small rock that shot out to the side, causing the stone to ping against the wall loud enough to reverberate in the quiet cave.

Damn. Her muscles locked and her breath barely eked out.

*Move.*

Inhaling deeply, her muscles finally engaged. Missy scurried forward with more care this time.

"Don't leave," came a deep voice from behind her before she'd had the chance to take ten steps.

Startled, she flicked on the light, and when she spun on her heel, the light landed on the man's face. What skin she could see, appeared unlined though his beard and dark tangled hair that brushed his broad shoulders implied he might have just shifted. That, or he was some homeless man.

He instantly lifted his hands in front of his face. "Hey."

She backed up. Missy hadn't meant to blind him, but he had startled her. She lowered the light to his chest and noticed he wasn't carrying any weapons. While that was a good thing, the fact he was naked was not.

With effort, she kept the beam above his waist, not wanting to chance glancing at his lower half. Fearing he might do something to her, she continued to move closer to the entrance.

"Where am I?" he asked, his words coming out thick as if he'd just awoken. He reached up and dragged his hand across his neck. His shoulders then slumped.

She'd have thought the answer was obvious: he was in a cave. The confused man stepped forward while she continued her backward movement a bit faster this time, all the while keeping her light on him.

"Wait. Don't go," he pleaded. Missy halted but said nothing, her heart pounding too hard. "This is a little bit embarrassing but I need some clothes. If you could find something for me to wear and leave it outside the cave, I'd be eternally grateful."

Really? Did he think she'd have an extra set of clothes on her? She then recalled a few stories her sister had told her about some embarrassing situations her mate had found himself in after shifting. Perhaps this man was merely desperate and in need of help.

It was decision time.

Trust him or run?

ZANEDAR THE HUNTER had never met a human who wasn't a shifter before, which meant one thing: he was on earth. Well damn. As far as he could tell, he had two choices: one was to tell this delicate creature the truth about how he came to be there and chance her running away, and the second was make up a story whereby she might give him some aid. Mentioning he was a shifter was too risky since humans weren't aware of his kind.

As much as he hated to deceive anyone, he had no weapons and no way to buy anything. Basically, he was at this woman's mercy. Without her aid, the next twenty-four hours would be harder than they needed to be.

Not wanting to scare her off, Zanedar stepped backward and his right leg buckled. Had he not reached out and grasped the rough cave rock, he might have fallen. Stupid injury. Hibernating must have triggered his bear's need to conserve energy and had shut down.

"What are you doing here?" she asked, her voice as strong as a steal blade yet as light and sweet as the finest wine.

*Truth or lie?* "I don't know exactly. My best friend just died, and I remembered deciding it might be a good idea to get stinking drunk. Apparently, I was mistaken. After that, it's all a blank." He waved his hand. "Somehow I ended up in this cave." He was rather pleased that he'd come up with that story, though much of it was true.

"I'm sorry about your friend." She continued to edge backward, and he couldn't let her leave.

"Thank you. I'm Zane…" Telling her he was called Zanedar the Hunter might scare her more than he already had. People from earth had two names. "Zane Hunter."

Thankfully, she stopped. "I'm Missy Berta."

He liked the rhythm of the name. He liked a lot more than that about her, but he needed to focus. Finding a way back home was his first priority. "Nice to meet you, Missy Berta. So do you think you can help me get some clothes? I'd hate to have to live in this cave for the rest of my life." Zane smiled, hoping to disarm her.

She lowered the beam of light so that it lit the dirt at his feet. "I guess I could ask my sister. Her husband might have something you could wear."

While doubt filled her voice, he was thrilled she considered helping him. He also was pleased she hadn't said her husband might have something for him, though he wasn't sure why he should care.

*She's your mate*, his still sleepy bear chided.

*You're wrong*, though if he were staying, he'd consider enjoying someone as delightful as this woman.

"Zane are you okay?" she asked, sounding worried.

He didn't need her to doubt his sanity any more than she already had. "Ah, yeah. I'm still trying to get my bearings."

"I said I could try to get you some clothes."

Wearing some made for the average man might be difficult. He'd been told most of the men here were smaller than he was, but he couldn't be too picky. "That would be great."

"I need to go outside to make the call," Missy said, her words hesitant, almost as if she was considering running. "The cell reception inside the cave is non-existent."

He wanted to question her about what she meant by reception, but that might lead to her asking him things he wasn't ready to discuss. "Okay."

When his sweet smelling savior turned around and rushed toward the light, he followed her outside, keeping a good distance behind her. All of the women he knew could shift and fight if they were scared, but human women, he was told, had no such skills.

When she finally reached the forested area and turned toward him, he couldn't help but stare at her beauty. He bet she had skin as soft as a doe's and her hair? Amazing. It was auburn, as the richest leaves of fall. Missy only came up to his chest, and while she wasn't slim hipped, he had no doubt he could have picked her up with one arm. Delicate women weren't something he often saw, but he definitely found her shape highly stimulating.

*I wonder why*, his snarky bear retorted.

Zane needed his inner bear to go back to sleep. The long rest must have addled his brain.

This intriguing yet feisty woman pulled out something from her bag that was rectangular and small. Keeping her gaze on the item, she ran her finger across the surface and then placed it to her ear.

Her eyes lit up a moment later. "Izzy. I'm glad I got a hold of you. I need a favor," she said. "I know you'll think I'm crazy, but as I was picking mushrooms for Anna, I ran into a man in one of the caves on the south side of town who lost his clothes somehow." She turned her back on him, but her voice still traveled. "I don't know if he is. No I don't think that would be a good idea. Just listen. All I need is for you to bring me some of Rye's old clothes. Or better yet, could you send Rye and maybe even Kalan?" She glanced over her shoulder at him and ran her gaze up and down his body, stopping briefly at his cock. It must have been the lighting under the canopy of trees, but he swore blue sparks shot off her arm. "I'd say he's six feet eight and quite thick. Thanks." She lowered her arm and faced him, still holding the odd device in her palm.

"Can you get the clothes?" he asked, needing to take his mind off this alluring creature. His body was slowly waking up, as was his cock.

"Yes. My sister said she was confident she could find something to fit you. It will take her at least half an hour to get here though." Missy lowered her gaze and sucked in a breath. "Your leg is cut. Do you need help?"

The unfamiliar sympathetic tone cut straight through him. Now that he was awake, he could heal the gouge that sliced him from thigh to knee, as well as the injury to his joints, but if it meant she'd stay around longer, he'd let her look at it. "I'd like that."

She opened the bag slung over her shoulder, pulled out something, and then immediately stuffed it back inside again. "On second thought, I probably should wait until my sister and her husband arrive."

Damn. She was afraid, but he had no idea how to let her know he'd never harm her. Zane actually had to work hard not to let his chest cave. To think he'd been so close to having her trust.

"No problem. It doesn't even hurt." He'd say anything to keep her there. To show her he was no threat, Zane slid down to the ground to wait for her sister to arrive.

Missy leaned forward, indecision crossing her face. It was if she thought he'd just collapsed. "Are you sure you're okay?"

Zanedar needed to keep his lying to a minimum. "I'll be fine. If you want to wait someplace for your friends to arrive, I'll just rest here." Resting was the last thing he needed right now. He certainly wasn't sleep deprived.

"They'll find me, but I do need to call another friend. I was here collecting mushrooms for a healing potion for her, and I need to let her know I'll be delayed."

Did that mean that Missy was a healer? Collecting herbs, coupled with her nurturing nature implied it. "Go ahead."

Once more she swiped a finger across the rectangular box, tapped it, and then lifted it to her ear. Zanedar really wanted to understand how she was able to communicate with another person without wires.

"Anna, it's Missy. How are you feeling?" She nodded and glanced off to the side. It was almost as if she was trying to decide if she should leave. "That's good. I'm calling because I got a little caught up at the caves, but I'll be there as soon as I can. Please rest. I'll see you soon."

He didn't think she was sounding any kind of alarm, which was good. He certainly didn't need her to call the authorities and announce that some giant, hairy, naked man was residing in the town's caves. His gaze lowered to the torch in her hand. The size and shape wasn't something he'd seen before. More and more proof was coming his way that his life as he'd known it was about to change.

Between the light emitting device and her fascinating communicator, he needed answers in order to decide his next course of action. Unfortunately, he had to keep his secret a little longer.

Missy leaned against a tree fifteen feet away and studied him. As long as he was in acting mode, he decided to carry his ruse a little further, mostly to see how she'd react. Zane leaned over, rubbed his scalp, and let out a slight groan, acting as though the blow from the fight still affected him. "I think I might have hit my head right before I passed out."

Missy straightened. "How long were you out for?"

He had no idea. That was the problem. "I'm unsure. Right now, everything is a bit fuzzy. I know this sounds crazy to ask, but what year is it?" She'd used the same *crazy* comment as an excuse for asking something out of the ordinary, so he thought it might work for him.

"It's 2017. What year do you think it is?"

Zane's heart nearly stopped. She had to be wrong, but to question her again would ruin things. "The same year."

Well damn. His situation was worse than he could have ever imagined.

**PACK WARS** (Paranormal)
Training Their Mate (book 1)
Claiming Their Mate (book 2)
Rescuing Their Virgin Mate (book 3)
Box Set (books 1-3)
Loving Their Vixen Mate (book 4)
Fighting For Their Mate (book 5)
Enticing Their Mate (book 6)

**MONTANA PROMISES** (Full length contemporary)
Promises of Mercy (book 1)
Foundations For Three (book 2)
Montana Fire (book 3)
Hart To Hart (book 4)
Burning Seduction (book 5)
Montana Promises Box Set (books 1-3)

**ROCK HARD, MONTANA** (contemporary novellas)
Montana Desire (book 1)
Awakening Passions (book 2)

**HIDDEN HILLS SHIFTERS** (Paranormal)
An Unexpected Diversion (book 1) – FREE
Bare Instincts (book 2)
Shifting Destinies (book 3)
Embracing Fate (book 4)
Promises Unbroken (book 5)

**SOUTHERN SHIFTERS KINDLE WORLDS**
Bear 'N Dirty

**WERES & WITCHES OF SILVER LAKE**
A Magical Shift (book 1)
Catching Her Bear (book 2)
A Surge of Magic (book 3)
The Bear's Forbidden Wolf (book 4)
Her Reluctant Bear (book 5)
Freeing His Tiger (book 6)
Protecting His Wolf (book 7)

# Author Bio

Want 3 FREE books? Sign up for my newsletter.

COPY AND PASTE INTO YOUR BROWSER:
http://smarturl.it/o4cz93?IQid=MLite

Check out my latest interview on You Tube:
youtube.com/watch?v=sQo5pyyVMDI

Not only do I love to read, write, and dream, I'm an extrovert. I enjoy being around people and am always trying to understand what makes them tick. Not only must my books have a happily ever after, I need characters I can relate to. My men are wonderful, dynamic, smart, strong, and the best lovers in the world (of course).

I believe I am the luckiest woman. I do what I love and I have a wonderful, supportive husband, who happens to be hot!

## Fun facts about me

(1) I'm a math nerd who loves spreadsheets. Give me numbers and I'll find a pattern.

(2) I just moved to Costa Rica and live on the beach!

(3) I also like to exercise. Yes, I know I'm odd.

I love hearing from readers either on FB or via email (hint, hint).

# Social Media Sites

**Website:**
www.velladay.com

**FB:**
www.facebook.com/vella.day.90

**Twitter:**
@velladay4

**Gmail:**
velladayauthor@gmail.com